The Templar's Treasure

by

Linda Lea Castle

The Templar's Treasure

Contact Information: info@thewildrosepress.com

Cover Art by *Tamra Westberry*

The Wild Rose Press
PO Box 706
Adams Basin, NY 14410-0706
Visit us at www.thewildrosepress.com

Publishing History
First English Tea Rose Edition, 2007
Print ISBN 1-60154-067-1

Published in the United States of America

Gair clenched his jaw against the grating sound of the lass's shrewish voice.

Everything about her was unappealing. She was slight and plain and the least likely maid to be blessed by the water of a weeping stone that he could imagine.

He would like to deny it, but he had seen what he had seen.

The stone had wept.

The lass must live.

There was no choice in the matter, yet each breath she drew chaffed his nerves, mind and soul, each insult burned his ears like hot coals.

By letting her live, he was betraying his brethren. It was an offense that could cost him his life—and his sanity if he failed to protect a lass—again.

Yet he knew that if Guiy, Raymond, Tristan, François and the others made a move to harm her he must and would face them all. She was blessed to do something wondrous for this land he loved and though his oath to the Templar's secret order was binding on his heart and soul, the preservation of his homeland was not something he could set aside.

He was in the center of an impossible puzzle. Either commitment made the other vow impossible to keep. And then there was the other vow, made in the hot sun with the stench of death in the air.

He had vowed to keep a lass a safe at his peril or his death.

He fancied he could hear God laughing in heaven.

He lightly touched his knight's spurs to Ibn Bey's side and urged him down into the deep, granite canyon. It did not do to dwell upon that which could not be changed.

The Lord had a sense of humor and He was not yet done jesting with Gair.

Dedication

For the Lord and His glory

The legend of the weeping stones was old. Some said the small stones incised with the crude thistle were hewn from the standing stones on Callanish. Others said it came from the ancient stone where Jacob laid his head when he dreamed of heaven. Whatever its origins, there was no disputing its power. From peasant to laird, most highlanders knew the prophecy of the weeping stones even if they didn't know where to find them, and they knew when the water trickled forth, they were in the presence of one who would be integral to the survival of Scotland. However, there was a sting in the tail of the blessing; whoever was so marked by the stone was fated to love only once, whether it be for good or ill.

Chapter One

1393, France.

"At last, the treasure is at hand."

The booming voice was barely audible over the fury of the storm battering the French mountains. Broad shoulders crabbed their way through the jagged opening of the slot cave, heaving and straining to fit through the narrow fissure. As the natural crevice widened, chisel marks appeared. Stonemasons had long ago hewn vaults beneath the cliff where the abandoned church sat lonely and unused.

The sound of shovels and hammers on rock echoed up from the hole that had been hacked into the stone floor of that holy place, and below, if the battered vellum that had passed from hand to hand through the long years was true, a cavern would be found—a cavern that held the treasure of Solomon's Temple. Gair raised his gaze to the seeping groined ceiling overhead, marveling at the engrailed crosses and fanciful designs. He wondered if he or any of his companions would live to rue this night's work. Water dripped down upon his helm, over his mail and finally trickled through cracks in the chamber floor. He muttered a quick prayer for protection, and for forgiveness—if one such as him could ever obtain forgiveness. Was there a limit to the sins God could overlook?

He tried to ignore the feeling of dread that enveloped him. A cold stab of unease pierced his spine, and he was overwhelmed with the urge to turn and leave this mysterious place. But his feet refused to obey.

Duty held him fast. He owed these men.

It had been two years since nine warrior knights had rescued him from a slow death. Poor Fellow Soldiers of Christ and The Temple of Solomon was what most of the world called them now. Not so long ago they were known throughout the world as the Knights Templar, originally sworn to the protection of pilgrims, before a king and a Pope had roasted them and declared them outlaw.

Gair called them all friends.

In payment for their courage and compassion, he had taken the temporary vows their mysterious order offered. He had bent his knee and his head, vowing to take up their cause as his own. He had followed them without question, to Cyprus, then France and beyond. Month after month, the knights had poured over ancient scrolls and rotting maps until finally, they had arrived at this forgotten location on a rocky hillside of France.

And only now, with a demonic storm howling and the drip of water on his face had he learned what they sought and why.

They were mad. 'Twas not only ancient secrets and holy relics the Templars coveted, but a lost treasure wrought by the faithful, brought to France during the first crusade—a mystical horde of items. He could feel the tension rippling among them. They believed the end of their quest was at hand. Gair's heart beat hard and fast, but not for the same reason as his companions. A part of him hoped they had found the treasure. Because when they completed their quest, he could return to his beloved highlands. Perhaps he would finally find a small measure of peace in the lonely hidden glens of Scotland. If not, at least he would have solitude. And there was a secret part of him that hoped the legend was no more substantial than smoke, for he feared what they might unleash if the treasure existed.

"We have it!" A gruff voice brought Gair's thoughts spinning back to the present. One by one, the warriors squirmed from the hole in the stone floor. They climbed from the cavern; their long, pale surcoats, emblazoned with a splayed crimson-cross, were covered in dirt. They fell to their knees on the rocky French earth beneath the groined ceiling to pray. When they were finished, they gained their feet.

"Make haste, Gair. We must load the treasure and make for the coast—with luck we will be soon safe in Scotland."

"As you command." Gair gripped the hilt of his sword

a bit tighter at the mention of home. "I pledge my blood in service to you. I continue to be yours to command until your treasure is safely hidden in the vaults beneath the Sanctclaire hold."

Rene, the eldest of the Templar knights returned to the hole in the floor. Within moments, he reappeared carrying a silver coffer. Beads of sweat dotted his hoary brows. "It is all there, just as they said. I actually laid hands upon one—." His voice choked and cracked. He shook his shaggy head, unable to continue. "Gair, you guard our backs while we bring it up. We will need to make more than one trip to bring it all to safety."

****

Rain fell in icy needles borne on a frigid wind. Scotland's gray and empty shore played hide and seek in the mist. This final journey from France had been rough, the seas unforgiving, and the winds uncooperative. At last, the heavy ship was in sight of land—and refuge.

Gair sucked in great breaths of air and willed his heart to slow its pace. He was coming home to stay. With this final load, he was finished. He could lose himself in the vastness of the highlands. He prayed he could forget his sins and that God would grant him peace. For months, Templar knights had been on the run, fallen from favor and declared outlaw heretics by a fickle church, hunted like animals by hired assassins. Gair had followed them, protected their backs, bled and fought at their sides. Still it did not wash away the guilt over her, which surfaced each time he closed his eyes for rest. He had witnessed too much horror, spilled too much blood. Now he lived only to complete his vow to the Templars and return to his beloved highlands. His temporary oath was all that remained of honor and integrity in a world gone mad with greed, superstition and the lust for power.

"Do not look so lost, *mon ami*." Guiy de Lombard spoke as he approached, staggering a bit before he steadied himself against the sway of the ship. The Florentine pilot that had taken them from the misty French shore trip after trip had proven to be an expert seaman. It had taken four years of clandestine voyages to remove the treasure. Now the same man guided the heavy ship through the narrow cove.

3

Choppy waters sent mist swirling around the masts while wind tugged at the sails. Waves crested, rolled and slapped against the hull, shoving the craft sideways.

For a moment, Gair felt as if he were no longer welcome on Scottish soil. The thought clung, wet and heavy to his shoulders, but suddenly, the ship lumbered its way to shore, fought its way back to the land that Gair loved—just as he had fought to survive, struggling to return to the remembered peace and beauty of the isle.

"We are at last here. Sanctclaire has promised sanctuary when we reach the stout walls of his castle. What we protect will no longer be in jeopardy. We will all be safe." Guiy sounded weary.

Safe. Within the strong walls of the Sanctclaire castle, the Templars could be physically safe—for a time. But was safety possible for that which they had brought? It needed to be cherished and protected. 'Twas holy and mystical, and held the promise of untold power to those who would use it for their own earthly glorification; but it could also be deadly to the faithful, as poor Rene learned after running his fingers over the polished gold. If any part of the horde came into the hands of Rome and the church, Gair knew no power on earth could hold them back from bloodthirsty dominance and conquest.

Could any of them ever be truly safe? But if it meant the loss of every Templar, and Gair himself, they would keep their vow to protect it. With their last breath, they would prevent the bloody churchmen from ever claiming any of it.

The ship lurched. Gair stumbled against the wooden railing, feeling the bite of his cold, brittle mail against his arm. He had been young and idealistic when he first sailed from these shores, before the world stripped the scales from his eyes. Now his soul was as cold and hard as his armor, his virtue just as tarnished. The sound of a horse neighing in fright brought his thoughts to something other than his damned soul. He clambered down the narrow, moisture-slicked ramp to the lower hold. Fourteen stallions and the last of a holy treasure had been loaded into the ship's hold under the dark cloak of night. Now, only one desert horse resided with the treasure in the dim confines below the waterline. The

4

others had been given in tribute to lords, lairds and knights of the Order from France to Cyprus, used as bribes, gifts and currency to ease their way through the labyrinth of obstacles between France and Scotland.

But this horse was special to Gair. Only he and one other had ever ridden upon his sleek back. And no power on earth would separate him from this animal.

He inhaled the scent of horse dung and leather. It mingled with the earthy warmth of the stallion's body—a good smell, a comforting odor.

"Be at ease, Ibn." Gair smoothed his palm over the velvety nose of the blood bay. A swinging oil lamp illuminated his great, dark eyes and the old puckered scar along his shoulder. His fingers skimmed over the aged wound while he spoke low Gaelic words. The horse shoved his muzzle into Gair's hand, snuffling, whickering softly into his palm. 'Twas a mystery to Gair that God could create such magnificent beauty in the bloody and savage world of the Holy Land.

"Soon, my friend," Gair stroked the silky muzzle. "Soon you will be able to run on the heath and breathe the clear air of Scotland. Never again will you feel the scorch of a desert wind or smell the stench of battle. I swear it."

****

The slopes of Ard Na Said were slippery with rain, the best time for Heather to find the tender mushrooms so favored by the innkeeper below the great castle. She crawled from one tussock of grass to the next, her fingers probing in the rocky soil, ignoring the rain dripping off the tip of her nose. The earth was pliable and she dug deep. A gasp of surprise escaped her lips when she plunged her hand straight down through the grass and roots into a hole that swallowed her arm up to the elbow.

"St. Andrew, protect me!" She jerked herself free of the dark fissure. Good sense bade her move on, but her never-ending curiosity bade her investigate.

"Mayhap 'tis Arthur's own resting place." She whispered to none but herself. Legends abounded about the great shoulder of rock that overlooked Edinburgh.

Ard Na Said; Arthur's Seat.

Legend said the king still slept there with all his knights and they would someday awake. Certainly, the shoulder of rock was riddled with strange caves and the like, and who knew what might sleep in that stony honeycomb?

Heather tugged a clump of grass away from the maw of the hole. She peered into the darkness. Gran had told her Arthur and his knights would waken with a clap of thunder and take up arms to defend Scotland. Of course, Gran had fanciful tales about most every subject, and as far as Heather could recall none had been proven—yet. Likely, this was just a rabbit's warren. No mere barefoot lass would be part of the waking of the king, even if it was storming, and distant thunder vibrated the hillside all around her. Heather was common as dirt and had no illusions about her place in the world. Still, she leaned near the hole and sniffed the damp loamy earth while a hundred questions buzzed inside her head.

"'Tis no musky brock's den. The smell is sweet and fresh and there is no sign of paw marks or hair." Heather reassured herself as she wriggled nearer.

The rain was falling harder now. If she had a dram of sense about her, she would find a dry place to weather the storm.

"A place like a bonny tight cave right here on the crag."

With a little scrabbling and digging, she managed to enlarge the orifice. Of course, it wasn't a big hole, but she didn't need a big hole, she wasn't much more than a bony midge, as her Gran used to say.

She slipped her head and shoulders inside. It was too dark to see much of anything but she was aware that the cavern stretched out beside her, large enough to accommodate her entire body with room to spare.

She sat on her haunches, staring up out of the hole. Her cloak was wool and tightly woven, but it was old and much worn. Under this deluge, it had soaked up the rain, pulling heavy on her chilled shoulders. She peered up at the sky where angry, iron gray clouds blotted out the sun. The storm had turned day into gloaming and showed no signs of letting up. But as uninviting as the mizzle was, Heather was reluctant to go farther inside the small cavern.

"A lass with a lick of brains would not be afraid of

crawly things when she is near to drowning in the rain."
She mumbled to herself. She turned her head and peered
out to survey the mountain and below it, the forest of
Drumsheugh. Nothing stirred. The animals had wisely
gone to ground when the rain started to fall. The basket
beside her was only three-quarters full of mushrooms,
wild thyme and garlic. Not nearly enough to provide her
with a coin. She needed to gather more when the storm
passed if she hoped to earn a crust this day.

She wriggled backward into the cave like a badger
entering its den. Standing on her toes, she could just
reach the lip where a shaggy tussock of tall grass nearly
covered the opening. No rain came in now.

"Now I know how the wild things feel." She
whispered to herself. "Warm and snug as a rabbit in a
warren." She smiled at the notion and adjusted her worn
cloak so it wouldn't pull so hard on her shoulders.

Many of the folk living within the walls of Edinburgh
thought she was a feral thing just like the rabbits,
badgers and wolves that roamed the deeper parts of the
wood. One or two had actually said as much to her and
then hurried to make a sign to ward off evil as if she
might conjure some dour event. What would they think if
they saw her now? Whatever it was, she couldn't imagine
they would treat her much worse than they had since a
winter fever had taken her Gran and her Mam. Few came
near her small black house on the crag; acting as though
it was somehow her fault the illness had felled them and
left her unscathed. Her only friends were the wild
creatures that bided on Ard Na Said and the innkeeper
who bought what she gathered.

She sighed at the pinch in her heart when she
thought about her Gran. The old woman always had a
kind word and time to spin a tale. Heather knew them all;
the stories of Arthur and Mab, all the legends of
Scotland's sacred stones, about how the isle's past and
future was written in Scottish rocks from the western
isles to the Lowlands.

Heather knew the stone of Scone held Scotland's
destiny, the standing stones of Callanish and Orkney held
its legacy, and the weeping stones scattered across the
highlands held its prophecy.

"Destiny, legacy, prophecy, just like Gran said." Heather knew the standing stones contained magic for those who had the power to open it, and she knew that the weeping stones heralded those who would love only one time in their lives and had the duty to save Scotland.

She wriggled to shrug off some formless sense of longing that crept over her. She envied those special folk blessed by fate to play a part in the fashioning and forcing of history. She wondered what it would be like to have a love so powerful and strong that a soul could only risk it once.

But she was a simple orphan lass not destined to do more than remember the tales and gather mushrooms and wild herbs within the forest of Drumsheugh, and since she was plain as wren she wasn't likely to ignite passion in any man.

Heather rested her chin upon her crossed hands and stared out at the small aspect of her world. Raindrops beat hard and steady upon the crags of Salsbury. Far off, thunder clapped and rolled through yon glens, echoing like war-drums. The turf was glistening like green jewels in the drear midday. She must have dozed for she suddenly jerked awake at a sharp sound.

A dainty black hoof appeared right before her nose, then another and another. Four nimble feet danced, squashing the wet ground into mud only inches from the entrance to her hidden location. "Zut! Desert bred and raised, Ibn Bey does not care for your, how you say?...soft Scottish weather? *Oui*?" A deep laugh blended with a roll of thunder. She couldn't see the speaker but there was a humor in his heavily accented voice.

"*Oui*, you speak the truth, *mon ami* but he iz not ze only one who tires of ze rain. Does ze sun never shine?"

"You have grown soft and complain overmuch." A deeper voice, flavored with a highland burr and the peppery bite of impatience, answered. "There is naught wrong with the weather."

A moment later great wooden wheels rolled into Heather's limited view. The cart sank deep into the soggy earth bogging down until it halted with a lurch and the dull whine of straining wood and metal.

Heather pitied the animals pulling that heavy load

and wondered why anyone would take to Ard Na Said and not the road below. 'Twas a dodgy track in dry weather and nearly impassable during a storm. Only she and the wild things knew the easy paths of Ard Na Said.

"'Tis no' far now." The canty Scot's voice announced. "Beyond the shadow of Edinburgh's great castle and the city walls and onto the deep glen where the monarch roams. The Sanctclaire laird's sanctuary is high and dry—he will have a roaring fire and a cup of something to warm us."

A loud clatter made Heather jump. She swallowed her squeak of surprise. A sleek horse fell before her wide eyes. His hoof had found one of the rabbit holes that dotted the landscape. The rider tumbled to the ground, a tangle of dark flowing cloth and the metallic clank of armor.

"Och, Ibn Bey, are you hurt lad?" A bulky pack that had been strapped behind the saddle came loose when the animal lunged to his feet, shaking off the dew.

"*Mon Dieu*! Iz his leg broken?" It was the voice that had complained about the Scottish weather.

Heather found herself unusually interested in the answer. She rarely had company on the crag and never such interesting visitors. Many mounted riders galloped near the hole where she was hidden, silent and unseen. Flashes of muddy hooves drove her deeper into her hiding place, and she prayed they did not step into her hole. She was not sure if these men were friend or foe and dare not risk being discovered. Her small dirk was no match for the long sword she had seen on the fallen rider.

Heather loved all things wild and wooly, but the horse that had fallen was of such quality and beauty, the like of which she had never seen. He was sleek as an otter with a coat the color of dried blood, tiny hooves and expressive large, dark eyes. His body was smaller than the great draft animals she was accustomed to seeing. Yet, there was no mistaking the power in his form. He reared and whuffled, dancing in impatience.

"Be at ease, Ibn Bey." The soothing burr was smooth as mulled wine and warmer than a peat fire in the winter. Not only did it calm the horse, but it bewitched Heather, bidding her inch forward. Still she could see bits and pieces of the tableau.

A sharp crack of nearby thunder sent the horse into a frenzied hop, and now he clearly favored his left foreleg.

A hinged metal gauntlet was stripped off and tossed aside, gleaming in the wet grass only inches from Heather's nose. Long fingers started at the animal's knee and worked over tendon and bone down the slender leg, finishing with an inspection of the hoof.

"He wi' be sound but he canna carry the load any longer. He lost his shoe when he stumbled." The Scot's burr told someone beyond her vision.

She wished she could see their faces—could see the face of the man who spoke like a burbling burn over bonny heather.

Muffled words were exchanged—some in another language. Fine booted feet walked to the fallen bundle and, with a grunt, hefted it from the wet turf. The roughly laced hide bag had come open on one side allowing objects to tumble out onto the dull, watery sun. There was a faint glint of silver and gold before it was all hastily retrieved, repacked and loaded onto another horse. The sky cracked, and the rain began to fall hard again.

"Go ye on to the sanctuary. I wi' hie to the blacksmith in Edinburgh. When Ibn Bey is properly shod and I am assured he is no' lame, I wi' follow."

"*Oui*, Gair. But have a care. We may have enemies on our trail. The luckenbooths and the fine guildhalls of the city will be watched."

"Do no' fash yourself, Guiy. I wi' join ye soon and I wi' no' be going to any craftsman save the smithy."

Another smatter of a language that Heather did not ken and they were off. The group of men with the heavy cart and horses moved off into the shimmering curtain of falling rain. Heather held her breath while the remaining man, Gair, they had called him, spoke to the stallion he called Ibn Bey.

A fine and couthy name for the bonny horse.

"Ibn, old friend, we wi' have a nice stretch of the legs. Nothing compared to the distance of the desert and there wi' be no battle at the end. I vow ye wi' get an extra measure of grain when we reach Edinburgh."

Heather craned her neck and managed to see a bit

more. She watched as gentle fingers rubbed over a wicked scar on the animal's shoulder.

"No more fighting for you my lad, we are finally home. Home to peace and God grant it, forgiveness."

She frowned at the man's words. He spoke to the beast as though it could ken. He, Gair, spoke like a Scot, but he was traveling with *ghalls*, foreigners. What was a man of his mysterious ilk doing on Salsbury Crag in the middle of a storm? Heather rose on her tiptoes and poked her nose closer to the hole. Ibn Bey—she loved the feel of the unusual name on her tongue—moved off at a slow pace being led instead of ridden. The stallion favored his front leg, his gait awkward and canted. She watched man and horse until they disappeared into the mist and the fringe of trees at the edge of Drumsheugh then wriggled from her hole and gathered her basket. She brushed at the mud clinging to the lower edge of her damp cloak. Her hair was soaked, plastered to her cheeks and neck. She was dirty and bedraggled and wanted to go to her home and have a wash before the fire.

"But I dinnae yet have enough mushrooms to buy a dram of something warm to drink or a loaf of bread to slake my hunger."

Her bare toe nudged something hard. She looked down to find a clump of mushrooms, their pointy caps pearled with raindrops.

"Och, I have more than enough now. Mayhap I will buy my sup tonight like a lady of quality. I shall sip hot broth before the innkeeper's hearth and look down my troon at any who give me a stare." She plucked the fat, pale, mushrooms, dropping them one by one into her basket. In a flash of lightning, she saw something else nearly covered by the thick, wet grass, the hard something she had felt with her toe.

A rough leather bag, water stained, darkened and weathered with age blended with the soil at the edge of the mushroom patch. The thin leathern drawstring had broken. A patina of dull silver winked in the next flash of brilliant light.

"Och, what is this?" She peeled down the wet edges of the bag. A simple cup ground out of streaky brown stone lay inside. It was devoid of design except for a thin rim of silver that had been bent crudely around its edge.

"The great bonny man must've overlooked this." She looked toward the gloom of Drumsheugh. Gair and Ibn had disappeared into the rain long ago. She could never overtake them even if he led the beastie all the way. If she was honest with herself, she didn't want to find them. She was more than a wee bit happy to have found the cup.

"Losers weep and finders laugh, as Gran said."

It was not often such bounty fell into her hands, but well worth the wait. Heather tucked the cup beneath her wild leeks, garlic and mushrooms. It was a long walk to the tavern on the castle road, and if she didn't start soon it would be full dark before she arrived. She shivered at the notion of traveling in the damp night.

"And I dinnae want to get the dregs and leavings at the bottom of the innkeeper's pot, so best I get to it."

Chapter Two

Gair was obliged to duck or clang his helm upon the low lintel of the public house. The rain beat against his back as he surveyed the room. 'Twas dry with stout benches and scarred tables scattered 'round. On the back wall, a rough stone hearth held a roaring fire that drove the damp away.

The common room was close, and thick with the odors of braised mutton, peaty smoke, wet wool and men.

It was the smell of Scotland. It was the scent Gair had dreamed of during a hundred sleepless nights. No sweeter perfume could be found in a hot desert oasis or in the aged forests of France. He knew, because he had searched for it, longed for it, craved it to the marrow of his bones.

Wooden pegs fit between the joins of the rough stones of the wall where many half-dry cloaks hung, but he dare not removed his and reveal what he wore beneath. He did tug off his helm, slipped it beneath his arm and threaded his way beyond tables and benches. Since he had parted company with the others he had felt the invisible burn of eyes upon his back. His senses had been honed in a hundred battles and even if he hadn't seen the man who followed his trail, he was certain-sure someone was behind him. "Welcome stranger." A portly man with a patch over one eye, tapping a fresh cask spoke over his shoulder. He swung the light wooden mallet and drove the tap into the oak barrel with a hollow thud.

"Will ye have a bit of brew? 'Tis well aged and full bodied."

"Usequebaugh." Gair laid down a coin, savoring the word on his tongue as much as he anticipated the smoky fire that would soon trickle down his gullet. He had sampled wines from high mountain vineyard grapes, quaffed beer brewed from sparkling water and fragrant trailing hops, even sipped the strange draught brewed on

Cyprus, but nothing in his experience compared to Scottish usequebaugh.

"Too wet to be out." The tap-man said while he poured out a dram of smoky liquid. "Better have a dram to dry out yer gizzard, eh?"

"Soft Scottish rain is the touch of a lovin' woman to me." Gair could not begin to explain how it soothed his soul to feel the hard stones of Scotland beneath his boots and the whisper of rain against his cheek. Or how he yearned for the peace of a faraway glen where he would not feel the burden of duty while he tried, and failed, to keep someone or something safe.

"Sit ye down by the fire and warm yer bones, mon. You ha' the look of a man far from hearth and home." The friendly proprietor raked him with his one good eye. Gair didn't even care that the man's hospitality was motivated by a desire to serve another dram of usequebaugh and pocket another coin. Whether 'twas false or true the words were a balm to the soul. Gair hooked a boot around a three-legged stool and dragged it toward the great hearth. He set the helm on the stone floor beside him. His gaze was drawn to the crackling red and gold flames and he gave in to the urge to stare hard at them, something he could never have done while fighting in the desert. A warrior who looked into the fire was rendered blind when he glanced away. To indulge in this ancient manner of woolgathering was a quick journey to an early death. But Gair was home, and for this short march of time, he was just another Scot sharing the comfort of fire in a stout, dry, public room while they all waited for the storm to pass.

There was no secret intrigue, no ancient promise, no burden of duty. For this moment in time, he was a man without kith, kin or obligation. He had no vow to fulfill, no oath to keep. For the remainder of this night he could simply be a man. And if on the morrow he was overtaken by the nameless, faceless phantom that sniffed him out like a hound to a hare, then he would deal with the threat, swiftly and without mercy. For now he set aside those thoughts.

With his back against the stone wall, he settled fully on the stool and enjoyed the heat. The hearth was enormous, built of rough-hewn stones and ancient mortar, fitted and formed, with a front ledge before it that was large enough to sit upon.

Gair hiked one boot up on the edge of the lip and within moments steam rose as the fire began to dry out the sodden leather of his boots. He watched the misty vapor rise while his cold feet warmed.

It was a bonny thing to sit alone with his back against the wall and have no care of spies, assassins and or zealots. Guiy did not think so, but Gair had been certain they had finally out-run them all—until a short while ago. Still, this was simply an ordinary public house, one of many below the great castle of Edinburgh.

In another fortnight, his vow to the Templars would be fulfilled. Honor would be answered and he would be free to go in search of an unoccupied glen where he'd never have to make another vow to anyone. Then he could sit each night in front of a fire and try to forget.

The door banged opened on a gust of wind, bouncing against the stone wall behind it. Gair's hand went to the hilt of his sword before he saw it was only a half-drowned child that stumbled through the door, escorted by a torrent of rain, the hair plastered to her head sleek as an otter's pelt.

"Ah, Heather, lass. I dinna expect to see ye out in such a gale." The one-eyed tap-man said.

"Angus, ye know I must gather rain or shine if I am to have a crust." The girl shivered like a drenched dog. A smatter of angry words erupted from the men at the nearest table when she showered them with fresh, cold droplets.

"Have a care and mind yer tongues ye blatherskites or ye'll be out in the rain." Angus shook his mallet at them. He smiled at the waif and his voice was soft when he said, "Go, stand by the fire, lass. Ye wi' catch a chill if ye dinna get dry. A dram of usequebaugh will bring a flush to yer cheeks and heat to yer blood."

She pulled a face at the men, lifted her chin a notch and worked her way to the thick oak plank where the tap-man served.

"Och, and I canna drink usequebaugh and eat as well."

"Heather, lassie, I dinna ask for coin for the dram."

Angus ambled across the puddled floor to pour out a dram. "What did ye bring me in yer basket today, lassie?"

"A bit of garlic, some fine mushroom caps and a few thick stalks of leeks." She rubbed her pale hands together in an attempt to bring the blood back into them.

Gair watched idly as the tap-man and the half-grown bairn talked of commerce and reached a price that neither pretended to favor. He had a notion this was a ritual observed many times, a merry jig betwixt friends.

It almost brought a smile to his lips, watching the child and the inn-keeper haggle. He had missed this land; he had missed thrifty Scots, and the sound of his native tongue.

He sipped the usequebaugh and let the almost forgotten melody of speech wash over him. It had been too long since he heard it spoken. Heather finally took off her wet cloak. It was then Gair realized she was older than he had first imagined. She was thin, almost gaunt, but a woman nonetheless. She hung the dripping cloak and returned to the hearth. Her tunic was threadbare and thin. The muddied, tattered hem skimmed above ankles fragile as a bird's legs. She sat cross-legged and child-like on the great stones that formed the hearth, her keen gaze on the basket, while Angus explored what was in it. Gair knew this lass was well acquainted with hunger and want. He tried to look away but something kept pulling back his attention.

As her hair dried, the color became more mousy. Water dripped from the ends, an occasional sizzle from the blaze demonstrating how close she perched to the flames.

"Ah, wild garlic, I see. I can make a fine venison broth with these braw greens." Angus burrowed into the woven basket like an old brock seeking a hare. "What have ye here, Heather?" He lifted something from the tangled nest of herbs. Gair swallowed hard and sat up so quickly his boot-soles hit the floor with a thud. His heart beat like a war-drum in his chest.

The bag in Angus's beefy hands had been well hidden since they brought it from the church vault in France. How had this half-drowned lass come to have it? Gair had been so sure they had evaded the trackers. Had his companions been set upon in the wood when they parted ways? Had any of them managed to reach the Sanctclaire Laird's refuge, or were they all now dead at the hands of the assassins?

"It fell into my hands on Ard Na Said." Heather chuckled. She was rubbing her hands and extending them to the fire. Tiny hands, pale with cold and callused from work. A poor Scottish lass's hands, like any others, but now cursed beyond redemption because she had the misfortune to pick up a leather bag and find a little stone cup.

Gair's belly clenched, but he forced himself to remain seated on the three-legged stool. He slid his hand to the hilt of his sword. All the tension that had winnowed away in these last pleasant moments returned to settle in the muscles of his sword arm. His shoulder was tight, his attention focused on the leather bag.

He was no longer a weary Scot seeking shelter at an inn. Now he was a hunter—a predatory seeker with a blood oath to satisfy.

"Well, now, this is a fine piece, Heather. Would ye sell it? I'll give ye good coin. Ye could use a new tunic or a pair of boots for winter." He nodded toward her bare feet, stained with mud.

Heather frowned and wriggled off her perch on the hearth. Angus would likely give her a fair price. She considered the offer—a bonny new cloak would be a fine thing to own. But she had a dry roof over her head and food in her pot this eve. Her cloak was thick enough to serve another winter and she had a pair of shoes at the cottage—tight and pinchy things, so old the leather was cracked, she dinna care to wear—but she owned a pair of shoes all the same.

"Nay, Angus, I wi' keep it. I ken the wee, braw cup 'twill look nice on my table with a sprig of heather in it."

Angus smiled indulgently at her. Then he shoved the cup back into the battered leather bag and dropped it into her now empty basket.

"Och, well, Heather, as you say, but if ye change yer mind. Ye know I am willin' to buy anythin' you bring me." He moved away from the basket, his hands full of mushrooms and wild herbs.

It was at that moment when Angus was gone and the rest of the patron's were minding their own business that Gair rose up from his stool and moved closer to the lass. He stood behind her while she warmed her hands. She was a wee thing, the top of her head dinna measure up to his chin.

"Lass, the cup must be returned to those who lost it." He whispered for her ears only.

She whirled and looked up at him. Her mean tunic let him see more than was proper and he felt an almost forgotten tug somewhere deep inside him. Small and underfed, her eyes were wide, brown and wary as a doe's. The basket sat an arm's reach away from her on the lip of the hearth.

"What do ye ken about those who lost the braw cup?" She asked in a whisper. Was this tall man's voice familiar? Had she heard that voice on Ard Na Said? It was familiar—wasn't it? She was unsure, after all a whisper was much different than full-spoken speech.

"I ken that cup can cause pain and death if 'tis no' returned. Give it to me and I wi' see the deed done in your stead. You need no' worry over it."

"Nay. 'Tis mine to do with as I see fit." Heather drew the basket with the cup inside nearer to her body. "Ye are a great stinking brute if he' think to steal it away."

Gair hardened his heart while he tightened his grip on the handle of his dirk. Conflict ripped him in twain.

"Please, lass, show sense. Give me the cup and forget you ever saw it." Gair did not wish to slit her throat, but that was the nut and kernel of the vow he had taken long ago; to slay any and all who laid eyes upon the cup or any part of what had been brought from France.

He had made a promise to God, and then he had given an oath to the Templars. If he slew this lass it would be another damning death to stain his soul. Too many deaths haunted his sleep each night, he did not want another on his conscience, but he could not let the lass keep the cup for even one more hour. If he could only get it away from her by some other means...

"Lass, give me the cup. For all the angels in heaven, *give me the cup now.*"

The violence and conflict in his soul must've reached his eyes for she shrank back blinking in fear. She stumbled and nearly fell. Her hand shot out to steady herself. Half-frozen fingers brushed a curious carved stone on the face of the hearth. 'Twas naught more than a small, rough, native stone with a wee thistle scratched deep into the surface. Within the blink of an eye, a tiny droplet of water pearled on the rough rock, grew fat and fell. Two more followed before she snatched her hand away from the thistle cut into the stone.

Gair's hand fell away from the dirk. He knew the pebble for what it was. The legendary weeping stones of Scotland were well known in the hidden glens where he had grown to manhood. He pinched his lips tight to stifle the moan building in the back of his throat. The tiny carved stone had revealed her to be one of the chosen ones.

He could not kill this lass—and yet he could not let her live.

He could not keep a holy vow without breaking a binding promise.

What was he to do? What could he do?

The fires of hell rose up around him and he thought he heard the laughter of fallen angels.

If he fulfilled his vow to the Templars then he thwarted the destiny of Scotland, for this half-starved, half-drowned lass with wary brown eyes was a special one, a lass chosen for some higher purpose.

Gair had seen many wonders as well as atrocities while he was away from Scotland. His soul had been stripped bare, left raw and wanting in the desert sun. For a time he feared he had lost his faith, he questioned himself and God. Now he watched the water still dripping from the spot where the lass's hand had touched, and he knew the old highland prophecy was true.

Here was proof—just like the proof he had helped bring from France.

How could he keep his vow to the Templars without slaying this lass? If he did, would he not deny Scotland her predestined heroine?

And then there was his solemn vow to God; As Gair lay dying in the desert he had sworn to keep any and all defenseless lassies safe, even if it cost him his life and his soul.

Chapter Three

Lightening ripped through the gloaming sky as Heather rushed out into the rain. Her cloak fluttered behind her while she hugged the basket to her middle and splashed unheeding through the puddles.

It was nearly full dark, the rain icy, the wind harsh. But she cared not for the fury of the rain and storm for it was nothing compared to the awful violence she had seen in the man's eyes.

What could put so much hollowness in a soul? She shook the thought from her mind and ignored the cold stinging in the soles of her feet as she ran toward the dark crag of Ard Na Said.

"Home. I wi' go home where I am safe." She promised herself.

****

Angus stood staring at the swinging door of his inn. "Whatever has possessed the lass?" Angus grabbed hold of the door and put his shoulder to it, struggling for a moment against the gusts of wind.

"She ran out of here without her coins or her dram." He looked at the tiny portion of usequebaugh sitting untouched on the wooden plank where he had put it.

Gair glanced back at the weeping stone in the hearth. Evidently, he had been the only one to see it. Only he was aware of the miracle, only he realized the tiny puddle was not from the rain. It stopped leaking as quickly as it started. The crudely carved thistle glistened with dewy moisture. The mystical drops had mixed with the rainwater on the floor and remained unnoticed by all but him.

He scooped up his helm, knowing where his duty lay and what he must do. "If you wi' allow, I could take the lass her measure of usequebaugh. She willna have gone far in this storm. She looked as if she could use something to warm her blood."

21

Angus looked suspiciously at him. "I dinnae—"

"You may trust me. I am well known to the powerful laird who bides not far from here at Rosslyn. He is Frere macon, my brother knight." Gair obliquely said the words known only to a few. That phrase, and a few others, had given him safe passage across Europe. He had been advised that this inn was part of their intricate network of safe places and that one-eyed Angus could be relied on and trusted if the need arose. His words had the desired affect because he saw the tension and the suspicion melt from the man's face.

Angus's good eye narrowed and he said, "Och, I dinnae know. Aye, ye can take this to Heather." Angus dipped behind the board and brought up a small earthen pot. He poured in the liquid and added a bit more before he corked it tight and put it into Gair's waiting hand. "And this as well." He tore off a part of a wheel of bread, broke some cheese from a chunk, wrapped it in a lightly woven cloth and handed it all to Gair.

"Take her this. She bides at the foot of Ard Na Said in a mean black house. Let your nose follow the smoke or yer eyes the trail of wounded creatures, either wi' lead you to her door." Angus chuckled. "Anything wild in need of love and mending eventually finds their way to Heather of Ard Na Said."

Gair pulled on his helm and donned his cloak, tucking the bundle under his arm. He ducked beneath the lintel and stepped into the pelting rain. He had been foolish to think once back in Scotland the danger would diminish. Violence would dog his steps until the Templar's plan was complete. And though he loathed the direction of his steps and his thoughts, he was bound for Heather's home, a hunter on the trail of prey.

Innocent and helpless prey.

What was he to do? He had taken a deadly vow—a blood oath to uphold a just cause. But the stone had wept when she touched it. The lass was part of an ancient prophesy of power and valor. How could he honor one and break the other?

And then there was his vow to God, made over *her* blood.

Gair shoved the horrible memory aside and walked

briskly through the rain. The blacksmith had promised Ibn Bey would be shod and ready within the hour. Until then, Gair was obliged to walk.

Puddles had formed in the deeply rutted track. Foamy, brown runnels ran from the high castle down the steep road toward the forests of Drumsheugh as the last weak rays of sun died.

He would find the lass and do what needs must. She wouldn't be the first blood on his hands and something dark and fearful in his heart warned she wouldn't be the last.

****

Gran had taught her how to measure the distance of the storm's heart. A flash of light and three heartbeats later a boom of thunder.

It was close, very close, might even be right over her small home.

The force of the rain stung her face and neck. The weight of her soaked cloak pulled hard on her shoulders, the tie cutting into her throat. She was weary beyond belief but fear spurred her on. Every rattle of branch made her start, every flash of lightening revealed spectral shapes and looming silhouettes that caused her stomach to clench in fear. She saw no one behind her yet she felt hunted. She prayed for a protector and thought of Gran's stories.

"Och, if 'tis the time for Arthur and his men to rise, I pray it will be tonight. I pray they will come forth and see me safe to my door." She swiped at the water in her eyes and another tale burst to life in her memory.

Gran had told her about the weeping stones of Scotland. How certain mystical rocks that had come down through the ages had the ability to weep. Heather had seen the droplets form beneath her own fingers, felt the warm water well beneath her hand. For an instant, her entire body had burned with power and portent.

"But I am naught but a poor lass who lives rough and wild. I am no fine lady to be chosen." The sound of a branch cracking halted her steps and her tongue. Heather strained to hear every sound, trying to filter out the storm, the wind, the pelt of the raindrops.

For a moment, she thought...no, she must have

23

imagined it. She tightened her grip on her little basket and slogged on, her feet numb from the wet mud oozing up betwixt her toes.

The wind keened mournful and low as it whispered through the forest. Here in the deepest tangle of wood and vine, the ground was not so wet and it was quieter. Heather could almost feel the burn of unseen eyes on her back. She whirled and searched behind her but there was naught but trees and droplets of rain.

"Goose." She shook herself free of the silly thoughts. She could not indulge in fear. Besides, 'twas only a short way through the bracken and gorse and the rough crop of heather that grew on the slopes and she would be at the door of her own wee house.

"A hot fire and a cup of broth wi' put me to rights." For two years now, she had nobody to share her fire or the story of her days. Since the time of Wallace, the Lord High Protector of Scotland, her kin had been bleeding and dying in a futile attempt to drive back the English, and she was the last of the line. There were no more braw men to go to battle for Scotland, there were no more strong lass's to bear sons and daughters. All her kith and kin were gone and the English were here.

She was the last. She was alone. But she had a roof and the herbs and food that God provided. She faced each day with the hope that perhaps she might eventually find a man who would not think she was too thin, or awkward or plain and that she might, by the grace of God, have a son of her own.

A darker shadow loomed ahead. Her eyes followed the line of her low thatch roof while her heart gladdened. She was home where she would be safe, away from the terrors of the city, and stones that cried, legends that made no sense, and strangers who whispered into her ear. She put her shoulder against the thick rough-hewn door.

An arm as hard as iron and just as cold clamped against her throat and yanked her back before she could enter the house.

"Give it to me." A harsh whisper demanded. "Give it to me now."

"If ye are intent on slitting my throat for my purse, ye are soon to know bitter disappointment." Her own voice was harsh due to the strong forearm pressed against her neck. She had wind enough left to speak, but just barely.

"I'm but a poor lass. There is naught in my basket but a dozen wild mushrooms."

"Dinnae lie to me." Gair growled. He knew there was something more in the basket. He had seen it. Why did she lie? Was she the pitiful innocent she pretended, or was a sinister force already at work here in the forest of Drumsheugh? "The tap man took the mushrooms but he left something else in the basket."

"I ha' no coin, ye cur, I left it at Angus's inn." He felt every fragile bone of her slight body as she squirmed against him and tried to bite his hand. Her efforts were little more than the futile struggles of a week old kit when pitted against muscles hewn in battle and seasoned by hardship. The icy rain had soaked clear through her modest cloak and into the threadbare tunic that hung just short of her bony ankles above muddy bare feet. She was so cold it wicked off her in icy waves, chilling him to his very soul. It was a cruel jest that this frail lass was to be his latest kill. The mighty warrior was now reduced to murdering innocents.

Was he any better than the corrupt hunters that followed him?

"Just grab her jaws in your hands and twist sharply," the dark predator's voice inside his head commanded. Her neck would crack like a dead twig. Her death would ensure the secret was safely stowed within the thick walls of Rosslyn Castle.

Yet Gair hesitated.

Hasty decisions, and the folly of youth, had brought him to that sorry crossroads where he'd nearly died a slow, tortured death. Only by making a vow to God and the Templars had he come back from the brink of madness. He could not go down that dark path again. However, he had sworn to uphold the order, to defend the treasure and to take the life of any who learned their purpose.

"Ye great brute." The lass kicked Gair above the knee and though it was little more than a glancing blow it did throw him off balance. Her slick skin and sodden clothes slipped in his grasp.

"Och, If I were a lad... "

"You would already be dead."

Two quick bursts of lightning illuminated their surroundings. She stared up at him with wide brown eyes, so innocent and fearful that his breath hitched in his chest. Terrified, and yet courage burned in her gaze.

"Ye! I know you from Angus's inn." She hissed through chattering teeth. Was it from the cold or from fear?

A hundred bitter emotions rushed through him.

How had he come to this? How had his dreams of glory and justice turned him into a slayer of maidens?

He held her arm but his grip was no longer firm or punishing. Thick clouds of doubt and old guilt pressed down upon him. He stared at the lass who stood trembling before him but he did not see her—no, he saw all the old ghosts he had tried to bury in the hot sand of the desert.

He saw the faces of the Templars that had restored him to health. He saw the treasure he had sworn to protect. He saw blood, sand, swords and he saw *her*. And among all of that he caught a glimpse of his own damned soul roasting in hell.

Gair had to move—had to uphold his vows. Just as he was bound to honor the tradition and prophecy of his country.

"Bloody hell, 'tis a fact I am no *diune-usale*." He roared more to himself than to her.

"Aye, a gentleman would no' follow a lass to her house, or try to choke the life from her!"

"'Tis true, and may I beg yer forgiveness?" He asked softly.

"I willna forgive ye for skulking in the rain like some feral beastie—."

"I wasna' asking forgiveness for that sin—I ask forgiveness for the mortal sin I am about to commit." He pulled the razor sharp dirk free from the leather scabbard with a metallic hiss.

Her eyes widened at the moment she realized it was too late to run and too pointless to struggle.

Chapter Four

Gair shifted his weight in the saddle and focused on the rocky trail ahead. The mantle of guilt pressed down on him like a stone. His shoulders ached with it, his belly soured from it.

Yet he had done what he needed to do.

After the deed, he had retrieved Ibn Bey, skirted the city walls and the great castle of Edinburgh, avoiding any who might have been up and about. All through the night he had ridden. Though he wanted a fire and a dry place if not for himself, then for the stallion, he had pushed on. And still he had felt as if a shadow dogged him through the night. He had seen no man, nor beast but he could not shake the certainty that someone followed him.

The rain had removed all traces of the wagon wheels and shod hooves of those that had come before him, so he could only hope they were safe within the walls of Rosslyn keep by now. Gair reined the stallion over the heath where his iron shoes would leave little trace. It would not do to be seen—not after what he had done at the wee stone house—to the lass on Ard Na Said. With luck, he would be inside the thick walls of the Sanctclaire hold before the deed was discovered. If not he would be drawing his sword sooner than later, for he knew the black cloaked mercenaries of the Pope had spent gold and used torture to sniff out their trail, and this latest sin would be much to their liking. In fact, it would likely earn him death tied to a burning stake.

Four long years he and his companions had either fought or fled, remaining hidden while transporting the secrets brought from the Holy Land. It was never a matter of if, but when, they would be found, when they would have to shed blood, when they would die.

Overhead a hawk cried and swooped upon an unsuspecting hare in the first gray and pink threads of pre-dawn. The rabbit's pitiful screams filled Gair's ears

27

and reminded him of the lass.

The lass of Ard Na Said had screamed.

Once. Only once. That was all he had allowed.

A fleeting pitiful sound of little consequence, it should have been a small matter after all he had seen and done, but he'd never forget the sound, or the look in her wide eyes.

Even at the last, she had not believed he would do it.

"The wee fool." He mumbled and shifted in the saddle again. He was not uncomfortable with the burden, but there was no help for it. So he clamped his jaw and set his sights on the far vale swathed in mist, just visible in the pinking streaks of coming dawn, where the treasure and his fate awaited.

****

There was a muffled sound. Heather could hear and that meant she was not dead—not yet.

Every inch of her body screamed with pain and a spot on her skull shrieked in agony. The stench of wet wool was strong in her nostrils, almost suffocating. Her ribs hurt and something hard and cold pressed against her back.

She could not move and yet she seemed to be moving, an odd disjointed sensation of motion.

She had the vague, foggy recollection of the cullion that had appeared from out of the mist and rain at her cot. His eyes had been cold and full of murder. The dirk in his hand had undoubtedly seen hard use.

The brute had tried to kill her.

She opened her eyes as the memory grew sharp and clear. The fog in her brain evaporated, burnt off by the fury she felt.

"I'm blinded." She blinked rapidly but naught but darkness followed darkness. "Lord above, I am blind."

"Yer no' blind, so cease yer wailin'." A deep voice answered.

She stiffened. She was being held with her back smashed against something hard. Him! He had kidnapped her.

"Ye clouted me in the head, and now I am blinded. The devil take ye."

"No doubt he wi' but not today. Cease wiggling before

Ibn Bey tosses you off yon cliff."

Och, so that was the reason she felt as if she were moving. She was atop the braw beastie. Never had she been on a horse before. 'Twas a heady sensation—one she would savor to the full if she were not hooded and bound like some hapless stag bound for the cooking pot. She was bound by her own cloak and the odor choking her was from wet wool

"I say cease your moving or I'll toss you off myself."

The threat was enough to keep her tongue behind her teeth. She froze, uncomfortable as the position was.

Pinpoints of light breached the worn weave. Not blind, after all.

Her ribs ached because she was being held snug up against the mail covered body of her abductor.

Her head hurt because ... he had hit her with the cairngorm on his dirk! He had struck her down! The cur, the fiend, the blackguard!

"Dinna curse me, lass, I tried to warn ye."

Had she spoken aloud or did the devil have the power to read her mind?

She did a quick inventory of her remaining body parts and was relieved to find them all still attached. What did he intend? If rape or murder was his goal he would have already done that.

Ransom?

She chuckled.

If that was his goal then the daft villain would be much disappointed. The foolish lack-wit had picked the poorest lass in Scotland! She was trussed up and captive like a capercaille bound for the fire but she could not understand why he had bothered because she had no rich relatives who would pay to have her back.

Surely even this dolt could ken that.

****

Time wore on while Heather mulled over what had happened. He had not slain her yet so she became a little bolder—not much, but a little. Bold enough to clear her throat and say, "Set me free, ye mangy cur." She knew he heard her because his powerful thighs tensed beneath her body but long moments dragged by and he did not answer.

"I called ye a dog—a mongrel—did ye no' hear?"

Silence was her only answer. He would not rise to the bait, so she heaved a sigh and sat unmoving on the horse, wondering where she was being taken and why.

Gair clenched his jaw against the grating sound of the lass's shrewish voice. Everything about her was unappealing. She was slight and plain and the least likely maid to be blessed by the water of a weeping stone that he could imagine.

He would like to deny it, but he had seen what he had seen.

The stone had wept.

The lass must live.

There was no choice in the matter, yet each breath she drew chaffed his nerves, mind and soul, each insult burned his ears like hot coals.

By letting her live, he was betraying his brethren. It was an offense that could cost him his life—and his sanity if he failed to protect a lass — again.

Yet he knew that if Guiy, Raymond, Tristan, François and the others made a move to harm her he must and would face them all. She was blessed to do something wondrous for this land he loved and though his oath to the Templar's secret order was binding on his heart and soul, the preservation of his homeland was not something he could set aside.

He was in the center of an impossible puzzle. Either commitment made the other vow impossible to keep. And then there was the other vow, made in the hot sun with the stench of death in the air.

He had vowed to keep a lass a safe at his peril or his death.

He fancied he could hear God laughing in heaven.

He lightly touched his knight's spurs to Ibn Bey's side and urged him down into the deep, granite canyon. It did not do to dwell upon that which could not be changed.

The Lord had a sense of humor and He was not yet done jesting with Gair.

****

Heather's mouth was dry and her bladder was full. She didn't know how long they had been traveling but it seemed forever. One part of her was sick with dread but another part of her, one she had never encountered

30

before, was exhilarated. She was surely far, far from her small house if the endless jostling of the horse was any indication.

She had never been away from the crags of Ard Na Said in all her born days. From rising at first light until the moment she found sleep, she lived her life within sight of that broody peak. It and the castle of Edinburgh on the top of the black stone cliff had been the boundaries of her existence.

Until this strange violent man came into her life.

She still wondered the why of it all. The only possible reason she could find for his strange action was the little stone cup in the leathern bag. But it was not gold—surely not worth so much that he would go to the bother of taking her away from her home. Or was she even more simple than she knew? Could the value of objects beyond her small world be measured by some different standard that she could not ken?

It was a puzzle that baffled Heather.

Just like the memory of the weeping stone at the inn.

It would please her to think that she was somehow borne to greatness but in her heart, she knew that was naught but a piper's sweet dream. She was born of plain-folk and she would die plain-folk. There was naught about her that was special—not special enough to fulfill the prophesy of the weeping stone.

Or was there?

Could that be the reason she now found herself in this odd dilemma? Did this man know more than she did? Had he seen the water well up and drip? Could that be it? Was he an enemy of Scotland? Did he know of the legend and think to change it?

But if that was true then he saw more in Heather than she saw in herself, for she did not believe she had the stuff that legends were made of. So she remained silent and turned the events over and over in her mind, but no matter how she looked at the puzzle she could not find a solution.

****

Gair was weary and he knew by the way Ibn Bey's delicate ears worked back and forth that he was tiring of this strange burden, only the third human to ever ride on his back.

Gair thought the lass might be whispering to herself, for the faintest of sounds came from inside her cloak. Was she crying? Did the stallion hear what Gair could not? The heavy metal helm he wore protected him in battle but it restricted both his sight and hearing.

It galled him, when he realized he was curious about her. He didn't wish to be, but it nipped at the edges of his mind. There must be something more to her than first could be seen. Perhaps she was truly high born and some calamity of fate had brought her to the sorry place where Gair found her. Maybe she was the by-blow of a noble— could even be the off-spring of the king, the result of a reckless assignation. A hundred unlikely but possible explanations flitted through Gair's mind. He was so occupied with the lass that he did not see the shadow that moved like smoke from tree to tree on wet leaves that carried no sound. He did not see the flash of metal in the bright rays of morn, or hear the faint twang of the bow when the arrow was loosed or the hiss of the shaft as it cut through the crisp air.

****

The path was steep, narrow and treacherous. Ibn Bey snorted while he scrambled up a loose scatter of stone. Gair's heart swelled with admiration for the little Arab. No matter the length of the journey, or the weight of his burdens, he trudged onward, determined to do what Gair bid. Every new land, each new peril, the horse had been faithful. Only Gair knew what the horse had been through—what they had both endured in the hot desert so far away. The long scar along his shoulder was healed but he couldn't help but wonder if the stallion remembered each night in dreams just like Gair remembered the scars upon his soul.

Ibn Bey was the greatest treasure Gair possessed but he had been bought with blood and death.

If not for the band of Templars, Gair would have died in the endless expanse of sand, his bones bleached and forgotten and the stallion would have died too. He owed them much, but his debt was nearly paid now. Only a little while longer and he would have fulfilled his promise to them.

****

The sky lightened until the glory of full dawn swept down the gorge to reveal a wild fell. At the apex of a majestic crag, a massive castle fortification perched on the cliff overlooking frothing burns, untamed forests and blooming heather. The castle was imposing and its legend stretched across the land, the sea and beyond.

"Rosslyn."

Gair's destination.

The great castle had been raised upon a shoulder of solid rock, and within the thick, protective walls, many levels had been hewn from within the granite mountainside. The keep was deeper beneath the ground than what was visible atop. A long stone bridge, wide enough to accommodate ten riders abreast, arched to span a deep chasm, one of two known entrances to the castle, while many more secret passages were hidden by stone and leaf. A waterfall thundered below Rosslyn while plumes of white water plunged down the cliff face, filling the air with damp and mist. In the early morning, a thick cover of fog hung like dragon's breath around the two round western towers.

It was massive. It was impregnable. It was the Sanctclaire hold.

At that moment, when Gair was overwhelmed with admiration for the architect and the stonecutters who had built such a place, he was overtaken by half a dozen mounted men. Their faces were grim as they surrounded Ibn Bey, halting the horse in his tracks.

"Where have you been? We have been saying prayers over your departed soul for hours." Tristan said.

"I was delayed. And 'tis fortunate because I discovered this." Gair withdrew the leather sack from the pouch he had tied behind the saddle.

"*Mon Dieu!*" Guiy rode closer. "But how?"

"When Ibn Bey mired in the mud. It must have fallen." Gair's voice was full of weariness. Now that he was here and the cup at last safe, his shoulders ached with the burden he had been reluctantly carrying.

"But what is this?" François Albemarle pointed at the cloaked bundle in front of Gair. "My brother, what have you brought among us?" François asked.

33

"'Tis is a small matter. I must speak with Laird Henry Sanctclaire about it."

Guiy frowned. "I wonder what it is you hide from us and why, eh?"

Heather stiffened within her cocoon of wool. She could feel the danger seeping through her cloak. The men were speaking in a rapid combination of English and French, some of it she could understand without really knowing the language because of the tone and tension in the air. She sensed she was in jeopardy.

If the villain Gair had not brought her here, she would be home before her own fire. He had much to answer for, this abuser of women.

"Och, Gair, do ye no' come and greet me when you arrive?" A loud voice demanded in a rough Scot's burr. The echo of it brought silence. Heather's own ragged breathing and the roar of a nearby waterfall was all that reached her ears for a long moment. Then there was a soft spoken word, a muffled reply. She strained to hear but she could only understand part of what was being said. There were more whispered words and then she heard a loud command.

"Take that to the lowest chambers where it will be safe. Take the other to the upper floors; I will advise my lady-wife you have at last arrived. She has been fashing like a mother hen who has lost a new chick."

Och, Heather wondered which direction was she to go—up or down? Yet she held very still. She felt Gair step down from the horse. In the blink of an eye, she was picked up and slung over a hard shoulder. The breath was forced from her lungs and she saw a shower of black stars before she was able to catch her air. She was being carried like a felled stag with his hand on her rump. It was yet another insult in a long list of insults.

"Make no sound, lass, for it may cost your life." Gair's gravelly whisper warned.

She did as he bid. For now. There would be a reckoning, she promised herself, later. He had much to answer for.

The sensation of being hauled upstairs jarred her bones. Finally, she was set on her feet. A shove to her chest sent her falling backward, she braced herself for a hard landing but instead found herself on the softest surface she had ever encountered.

"What? Where—" She spluttered.

Gair frowned at the lass and pulled the cord that bound her cloak around her. He had brought her to a finely appointed upper chamber where a roaring fire had been laid. Beside it, a great oaken tub of water was sending little clouds of vapor into the air. No doubt, that would have been his bath if not for this lassie. He sighed and quit the room, his thoughts now on Henry Sanctclaire. He wasn't sure what Henry would say when they met in the hall as ordered, but at least he had agreed to listen to Gair's story before he passed judgment.

Gair entered the seat of the Rosslyn laird to find the Prince, as he was often called, sitting in a huge carved chair on a dais, glaring at the half dozen men before him. He rubbed his thick, reddish beard while his pale, shrewd eyes flicked over each one in turn.

He was a big man, tall, raw boned with a nervous energy that infected all around him. Right now, that energy rolled off him in waves of disapproval and barely restrained anger.

"Tell me what has led to this sorry pass." His voice was soft and gentle, surprising considering the fury in the gaze he trained on Gair. "We have all agreed, Gair. There is no exception. Anyone who cast eyes on even a hundredth part of the treasure must die. Ye know this. Ye took a blood oath."

"He broke his vows." Tristan Carillon, high-born son of a French nobleman, accused, his knuckles white from gripping the jeweled hilt of his sword.

"I promised to hear Gair's story and that I wi' do." Henry cast a look at Tristan; the knight clamped his lips shut.

"I returned the cup." Gair said simply. "It is now safe with the rest, hidden in the deepest cave of Rosslyn's crypts."

"Och, Gair, dinnae act as if you are addled of wit. I ken you found it but what about the lass? She has seen it. If the black-robes should get their hands upon her— torture can loosen any tongue." Henry said.

"She had found it on the crag, fallen from the wagon

in the rain. She has no idea what it is, or the value of it. I only happened by chance to be at one-eyed Angus's alehouse near the castle road when she came to sell mushrooms to the publican."

"Which does not tell me why you brought her here? We have all taken the vow, though you and I are on a slightly different plane than these good knights, Gair, our oath is no less binding. You know what we guard. You understand the calamity that would blight the world. No one shall see any part and live. By bringing her here you have not saved her but only delayed her death." Henry's voice was taut, under steely control, his hand clasped tight upon the hilt of his dirk as if he might rise and see to the deadly deed himself.

"I canna spill her blood nor could I risk those who follow us finding her and bringing her to harm." Gair said. "The lass must survive. I must and will give my life to see her safe."

Henry's eyes narrowed and the other knights sucked air in surprise.

"Ye would defy me? 'Tis suicide you are bound for if you have fallen in with those who oppose us. I would know what has bewitched you, Gair, what has turned you from your purpose?"

"I havna' strayed from the path. I have given my oath to do all in my power to aid you and the Templars but I will allow no man to harm the lass." Gair said with more fury than he intended.

Henry leaned forward, his eyes pale slivers of ice, his fingers tight on his dirk. He asked, "Why?"

"Because she touched a small, worn stone in a public house near the castle of Edinburgh and it wept, my laird. It shed tears like a grief-stricken lass. She only had to lay her fingers upon it."

Chapter Five

"Are you certain?" Henry shoved himself up from the chair. He stalked down the dais, his heavy embroidered tunic with the Sanctclaire's heraldic device of a sea-serpent's head, its throat bound by a crown, glinted upon his chest. His fine boots rang a dull tune on the floor. He halted only inches from Gair's face. Of a size, he looked into Gair's eyes as if he could see the future in their depths.

"There is no doubt?" Henry's voice was soft and full of awe. "Truly the stone shed water?"

"No doubt"

"By Saint Kessog!" Henry slammed his fist into his other palm. "I never expected it to happen in my lifetime. Tell me more."

Gair nodded. "It was just as the legends say. The stone was no bigger than my hand, with a small thistle carved into it. 'Twas mortared into the front of the hearth at the public house. I have no doubt a hundred people must touch it each fortnight. Yet the lass had only to rest her fingers on it for a moment and the water came forth in copious droplets. She snatched her hand away and it began to dry up. The lass was shocked by it, as surprised as I myself at the sight, but she knew what had happened, I saw it in her face. She fled as if ten demons were on her heels. I knew she had the cup and I followed, intent on doing my duty, but I couldna'. Ye ken the reason why, my laird?"

"Aye, I see and I ken. Of a certainty, this changes your oath. You canna harm the lass. You were right to bring her here." Henry clapped a hand to Gair's shoulder. "But did you no' think to tell me what had happened? I would gladly offer aid for Scotland's future." His burr became thicker with emotion. "You do me no credit to keep such a thing from me, Gair."

"I had little opportunity to tell you." Gair said dryly

casting a glance at the knights who still glared at him. "They dinna ken—they still do not realize. They are no' Scottish. I couldna' tell you there and then and take a chance she might have been injured." Gair watched Henry Sanctclaire closely.

Henry turned and looked at the knights. The tension in their shoulders was evident, the anger and confusion in their eyes apparent. Suddenly a grin split his full beard, the skin around his pale eyes crinkling in merriment.

"Och, I forget that most of the knights are no' fortunate enough to have been spawned in Scotland. You poor benighted fellows of France were no' raised up beside the lochs of Scotland so it is no' your fault you dinnae know the legends and prophesies of old." His chuckle softened the good-natured insult.

"*Mon Dieu*, I do not understand you Scots. You speak in riddles and break blood oaths as if they are nothing but smoke." Guiy spat out the words. He paced a bit then whirled to trace his own steps.

Henry raised a hand. "For you, Guiy, I will try to make you understand. You and your order have done much that I admire but we Scots have strong traditions and old ways. Our customs go back to the earliest times. The stones of Scotland have endured since the very beginning of time, and they have power. When you set foot on Orkney, you will see the standing stones, but we have others as well. We have stones that weep and we have a stone that is used when we crown our kings. Our customs are strange to you, our legends may seem foolish, but to us they are binding and real as the treasure that bides beneath our feet. One legend is older than time, precious to we who roam the glens and fish the lochs. Ancient prophecy tells us any lass or lad of Scotland that touches a stone and brings forth water is destined to be one who keeps our land safe and whole. To kill one so blessed would be a sin none among us could contemplate or allow."

François glowered at Henry, his dark eyes narrowing. "So you have brought among us a monster sacré, a sacred monster? This woman, who you believe must not be harmed? Who is this maiden you so revere but who has the power to bring us all down?"

"She is simply, a poor lass." Gair said. This information made François openly bristle. He opened his mouth but was cut off before he could speak.

"Henri is our protector. We must believe him. I only hope he is not part of a *folie et deux*— a madness for two." Tristan said, casting an accusing gaze at Gair as if he were the one who had brought an affliction of the mind upon Henry.

"*Oui*, if it were any man but Henri Sanctclaire of Rosslyn telling me this fable I would suspect they were *faux devot*, you know, falsely devout, but if you, my Prince, say you believe this... this..." Guiy gestured in the air as if the word could be snatched from the ether.

"Prophesy?" Gair provided through clenched teeth.

"Ah, as you say, this prophesy, then we must respect that it is true." Guiy arched a brow. Although Tristan, Raymond and the rest nodded in agreement, Gair could see suspicious speculation remained in their eyes. He would not rest easy beneath the Sanctclaire's roof—not until the fleet sailed and the treasure no longer shared space with the gifted lass. When they were all gone and she was still here in Scotland, then he would believe she was out of danger.Later when Gair and Henry Sanctclaire were walking the battlements overlooking the deep wooded glen, and all the rest of the castle were preparing for the sup they would share, the Laird turned to Gair and said, "Tell me of the lass." There was an eagerness in his words that Gair had only seen present when Henry was talking about preserving the treasure. Then his face hardened and his brows drew together in a deep frown. "—And tell me how you could risk harming her by clouting her in the head?

Gair halted his steps so abruptly his sword blade knocked painfully against his shin. He grimaced against the unexpected pain, grabbing the hilt to stop the motion.

"Now it is you that does me no honor. I swear upon the Holy Rood I did no such thing. I wouldna' strike a woman for any cause."

"Then how did she come to have a great lump and tears up when my lady wife asked how she left her cottage. She has sent word to me that the lass believes you tried to slay her and failed."

Gair snorted. "If I had wished her dead, then dead she would be, but so far I have slain only one woman." The words were bitter as gall. He turned and stared out at the glen below, but all he saw in his mind's eye was blood and sand.

Henry stepped up beside him. "Gair, I'm your friend. I would listen should you wish to unburden yourself of this guilt," he offered, his voice full of sympathy and friendship. "Only God can do that, Henry."

"But only if you accept the forgiveness he would bestow. Perhaps if you speak—"

Gair whirled to stab Henry with his eyes. "Nay, I will never speak of it. Not to you—not to any man."

Henry held up a hand. "As you wish. Then tell me more of the lass who now bides under my protection."

His words were brittle, and Gair knew he had come nigh to offending the Sanctclaire laird but he turned his mind from that and thought of the lass. Heather of Ard Na Said, wet, frightened and vulnerable, that was the image burned into his mind, the way she appeared moments before he took her from her croft.

"She was terrified when she saw my dirk. The lass swooned and struck her head upon her own stone hearth. 'Twas not by my hand she shed blood."

"Och, and she yet she believes you hit her—she told Janet as much."

"The lass is burdened with too much imagination. Struth, there is little to recommend her. She is a scrawny rack of bones. Her tongue is sharp, and her wits are addled." Gair felt the old guilt and the new regrets mingling in his blood.

"She is not what ye expected and now she has sore wounded yer pride. And so have I, I ken." Henry smiled when Gair snapped his head up to glare at him. "Tell me, Gair, does she complain overmuch?"

"Nay." The answer was bitten off.

"Did she mewl or cry?"

"Nay. Not even when she thought I intended to slit her throat though evidently she has branded me to be a great blackguard with no honor, a loathsome cur capable of harming an underfed lass with no father or brother to protect her."

"Yet if the stone had not wept you would have slain her?"

Would he? Gair didn't know, and he thanked God the stone had wept so he hadn't been forced to face the horrible monster that lived inside him. He was certain he would run mad if another innocent lass's blood was on his conscience.

Henry clapped a hand on Gair's shoulder. "But ye are disappointed in Heather of Ard Na Said, I can read it in your face and your voice. Tell me why this is, Gair?"

"I expected one of the chosen to be extraordinary. I expected heart and courage, or in the case of a lass, that she would be fair of face and form, the finest that Scotland could breed. Heather of Ard Na Said is not special in any fashion I can see."

"True she is no bonny lass. Do ye think that makes her less deserving of her fate? I ken your treatment of her was rather less cordial than any lass would expect. And yet you say she did not weep. She did not beg for mercy. She endured her circumstances and now shoulders the burden of her surroundings with a quiet strength—or so I have been told by my lady-wife and her maids.

Gair frowned and considered Henry's words. Mayhap there was something special about the lass that did not meet his eyes. If she wasn't a beauty, then perhaps she was possessed of a keen mind. But Gair was still bruised by her belief that he had hit her. And in realizing that fact, he was suddenly swamped with sharp resentment. He had nearly fulfilled his temporary vows to the order and would soon be done with this burdensome quest. But with Heather's life hanging by a slender thread he had a new cause that would keep him from the peace and serenity he sought each night.

He had saved her. God had brought Gair to the maiden to protect her. The least she could do was show a proper degree of gratitude.

He had good cause to dislike the lass, he told himself. More than enough reason to resent her. And only one binding reason to keep her safe. The legends learned at his grandfather's knee were real and vital and impossible to set aside. So while he stood in the misty gloaming of Rosslyn, he closed his eyes and asked God to give him the strength he needed to keep this lass safe—and not let her die like the last one the Lord had entrusted to his keeping.

****

Heather stood stock-still, embarrassed to be tended by Janet Sanctclaire and her serving women. She had never been naked before anyone but Gran, and the oddest thing was the women hardly seemed to notice.

"Och, lass, but you are little more than bones. A good joint and breaking yer fast with oats of a morn wi' put some meat on yer. Why, when my Janet was a bairn I didna' let her begin a day without a proper serving of oats."

"Moira, you needn't bore Heather with tales."

"Tales, is it? Truth, be more like. And why shouldn't I be telling her? I raised our lady here. From the time she was a bairn until Lord Henry saw her. She was my darlin'."

"Moira, pray do not—" Janet was forced to stop speaking when the wrinkled old woman simply continued to speak. Heather had never seen the like.

"No man could find fault with Janet Halliburto, I will tell you that for nothing. She was considered a great beauty, but that was not why Henry had paid court to her at Direlton castle—'twas not the reason he had thundered around on his finest garron, wearing his best plaid, preening like a peacock, hoping to catch her eye. From the first time he saw her at Haakon's court in Norway, he had loved her because she was sincere, constant and her smile was like the dawning of the sun. And didn't I teach her that? A good heart and a kind soul—I always say. You have that look about you, child, that and something more, I'm thinking. Aye, bide awhile here, and I trow you will have a twinkle in yer eye and the bloom of roses in yer cheeks."

The door opened abruptly finally putting a halt to Moira's speech. A red-haired lass glanced up in alarm, skidding to a halt when she saw Henry Sanctclaire enter the chamber. She dropped into a clumsy curtsy, her arms full of muddied rags.

"Mi'laird." She murmured, then snatching up the cloth, hurried on.

"Henry, how wonderful to see you." Janet came to him, dipped into a quick curtsey and then rose up on tiptoe to plant a most inappropriately intimate kiss upon his lips. Heather felt her cheeks flame. She had never seen such tenderness before, it embarrassed her but some inner part of her also felt a tug of longing to see such closeness betwixt a man and a woman.

"Come see what I have done and tell me if you approve." Henry allowed his wife to tug him forward. She grinned at him and a world of meaning passed between them. They needed no words to communicate, Heather sensed.

Henry wore a dour Scot's face while he surveyed her from head to toe. Her stomach knotted with tension. She had no notion of what he would say. Would he be angry that his wife and her maids had bathed her, dressed her in finery as if she was some high-born lass instead of simply Heather of Ard na Said?

When she thought she could stand it no longer he bowed slightly at the waist and said, "I approve of both the lass and the gown."

Janet was busy straightening a bit of lace here, a fold there. She did not even look up but nodded and said, "Aye, the color does much more for Heather than for me. I am making a gift of it." She finally did glance up then and added, "With your permission, my laird."

"You have my permission and approval. Gift her with a few others and I will bring you new cloth from Orkney upon my return to replace any lack it leaves in your wardrobe."

Heather's knees were weak as water. Relief flooded through her.

"I will leave you now and see you both at supper. And Heather, I hope you will be comfortable here in Rosslyn."

"I thank ye, but I willna' be staying long. I will be returnin' to return to Ard Na Said as soon as I am able."

Henry's smile wilted. He drew in a deep breath. "Lass, I must insist you enjoy my hospitality for a good, long while."

"But—"

"There are reasons aplenty why you must remain here." Then he turned and left before she could question or gainsay him on the matter.

****

Gair rinsed his freshly scraped face with icy cold water from the ewer in his chamber and dried his cheeks on a length of huck. With his mail stripped, his sword and dirk laid aside, he knelt and prayed wearing only his small clothes and a simple tunic. He asked God to bless the land, his laird and the quest. He stopped the prayer just short of asking for the sweet release of forgiveness. It had been years, but he still felt responsible and undeserving of forgiveness. Almost as an annoyed afterthought, he prayed for the sake of the lass.

"Amen."

He rose and dressed in his customary garb. When he was finished, he donned only his dirk for no guest ever brought a claymore to table. He tossed on his long cloak and pulled it closed in front.. Then with grim determination, he started down the stairs to the dining hall. A strange sense of foreboding would not be banished from his mind as his spurs rang against the stone treads.

"It is all Heather's fault." He grumbled. She had been nothing but trouble since he laid eyes upon her, and he had a feeling nothing was going to change. But did that not signify he had a second chance in an odd turn of fate, because here was another lass who needed protecting, and perhaps this time he would not fail. A strange chill had entered his bones, almost like a portent of doom. He paused on the turnkey stair and moved to the nearest arrow-slit. Sunset was painting the world with a crimson brush. He scanned the hillside, the clumps of heather, the trees looking for anything out of the ordinary. Twice he did this. Twice he saw nothing. Yet his heart beat hard and slow in his chest.Someone was out there. Someone was watching. Gair could feel it in his bones

****

Hassir Ibn Falad Rashid sat on his haunches and stared up at the night sky. He had tried approaching the great citadel from every side but it was well defended. The gorge before him was a sheer cliff, dotted with caves and treacherous looking waterfalls that roared like the desert lion. On the remaining three sides, hidden amongst the trees and vines, were ingenious, almost invisible man-traps and sharp-eyed sentries with vicious looking axes and blades.

He smiled and rubbed his fingertip on the small beard that graced his chin.

By Allah, the man who commanded this fortress was blessed not only by a rich land full of game and many faithful men to guard him, but by an intelligence Hassir could only compare his accumen to that of the oldest and most respected desert tribesmen. His foe had chosen his friends wisely but it would not be enough to spare him.

Pulling his garment tight around his shoulders he crept into a cleft of rock he had found. He wedged himself in. It would be cold but it would be dry. Tomorrow he would continue to probe the defenses and eventually he would find a weakness—for even this man will have a weakness.

"Enshallah."

If Allah wills it.

****

Gair entered the great hall to find a fire blazing. The room was warm but did not banish the chill from his bones. Even though a dark worry nipped at his mind, Henry's hall engaged Gair's attention. He would never tire of the sight of it.

A great set of Scottish stag antlers graced the west wall. On the East, North and South were fine artistic displays of swords, shields, claymores, dirks and Norse war-hammers—sharp as hound's teeth and ready to be ripped down and taken into battle.

The Sanctclaire crest of a great sea-serpent girded by a crown and restrained by a short chain, was carved from one disk of solid oak, painted and displayed over the hearth which was large enough to spit and roast a full grown boar. Iron torches burned bright in every corner.

No Sultan's richly furnished palace or seductive harem could compare to a Scotsman's keep with a loving wife in residence.

Gair was standing in the arched doorway, staring up at the groined ceiling, marveling at the skill of the masons who had carved it out of living stone, when Henry approached from a recessed corridor that descended from above.

Rosslyn was riddled with passages, secret rooms and hidden entrances. The lower levels were a warren of vaults and caves. One canny entrance was located at the bottom of a dry well.

"Gair." Henry had Janet, his wife, on his right arm but on his left was a high-born lady, or so Gair thought until they came nearer and the iron torches illuminated her eyes.

He would never mistake those eyes. But his mind rebelled at the sight of her, for this could not be Heather of Ard Na Said—surely this was a changeling dressed in a snowy white gown with red fox fur around the collar and cuffs. The flowing gown emphasized her long neck and trim, lean form. Her beauty did not rival that of Janet Direlton Sanctclaire but she no longer appeared half-starved and wanting. She had something his traveling companions would label *je ne sais quoi*, an indescribable quality that was impossible to explain and just as impossible to ignore.

She descended the carved stone steps on little slippered feet that made no sound. Her mouse brown hair was shiny, clean and dressed with a delicate strand of seed-sized pearls in a style Gair assumed was the latest mode. He had never been one to seek the company of women, his one lapse of judgment in that arena would haunt him unto death, so he was ill informed as to fashion. But Heather was much altered.

Only her eyes were unchanged.

He swallowed an awkward breath at the sight of those brown eyes, accusing, and aye, damning him for bringing her here. He saw the faint, mocking smile that plucked at Henry's lips and the twinkle in Janet's discreet gaze.

They were enjoying themselves at his expense—laughing behind their eyes over a matter that was deadly serious.

Gair realized he was staring and checked himself but it was too late, they had seen his soft underbelly.

Heather watched the hulking brute that had captured her while his gaze roamed over her fine clothes. She knew the moment he recognized her as his victim, for the color had drained from his haughty, braw face. It was delicious, just as Janet Sanctclaire had promised. The kind lady had persuaded her to submit to a bath—naked and scrubbed by strangers!—and the careful grooming of her hair, to beard the lion in his den, she said.

Heather wasn't altogether comfortable in this finery but she did admit that seeing Gair-the-brute,silent and ill at ease was worth the tugging, pulling and lacing to which she had submitted herself.

It was a small pleasure but she savored it all the same.

She was caught unaware when Laird Henry Sanctclaire, whose name and reputation was known even to her, handed her into a tall backed chair. Her hands were shaking and it took every ounce of her control to keep her gaze steady, but she vowed to the Lord above, she would nay look away from Gair's eyes before he did. Finally, blessedly, he did just that, letting his gaze slide away.

She breathed a sigh of relief and focused on the lovely silver candlesticks and other finery on the table. It was far grander than she ever imagined. She had no time to worry she would shame herself during the meal, however, because a loud clamor erupted when a group of men entered the great hall.

Gair's eyes narrowed and Laird Henry, though he continued to smile, stiffened. His easy manner became closed and guarded. Even his wife seemed a wee bit nervous, as though a hungry wolf crouched in a corner of the room, waiting to leap.

Heather followed their gazes and watched as each man stepped into the hall, illuminated by the torches and a great iron circle holding dozens of candles suspended from the rafters. The flames of the fire in the great hearth reflected on the warrior's snow-white tunics. Each was emblazoned with a crimson cross with splayed ends.

"St. Andrew, preserve me, they are Templars!" She spluttered before she could bridle her tongue.

Lady Janet colored and lowered her gaze. Gair's stare returned to her face, and she felt the icy chill of it when he suddenly shoved back his chair and stood. Staring at her with cold intent, he threw off his cloak to reveal his tunic beneath. Heather saw the same device emblazoned on his chest.

"You! A Templar." She spat it like a curse and rose slightly from her chair with her palms flat on the table. "I should have known. But what evil have I done to invite the wrath of the Templars?"

"Be at ease, lass, here you are safe." Henry promised but she would have none of his assurances as her temper rose. Her tongue, once loosed would not be tamed.

"I have heard many tales of the heretic warrior knights, each worse than the last. In one-eyed Angus's tavern, it is said they secretly worship the devil. Other men swear the Order practices unnatural acts. I dinnae ken what unnatural acts are but I heard old Angus say King Robert the Bruce took aid from the Templars at the battle of Bannock burn, and was obliged to offer them refuge and was excommunicated for it. Angus said the Order died out but these dour men seem lively enough to me—"

"*Mon Dieu*, we are painted with the black brush by the wagging tongues of your country, Henri. Worship the devil—bah! And our unnatural acts are to pray daily and keep away from loose women." François said. "Now we are insulted by this...this, infant!"

Heather blinked at the fury in his retort. She clamped her lips shut but her mind was still running in circles.

What did it mean? A Templar knight had wrenched her from Ard Na Said. And if as this Frenchman said they shun the company of women, then why was she here? Certainly the Templars were shunning her now. They had moved in a group to the farthest point the table would allow before they took their seats. She had a notion that if it would not have offended their host they might have taken their meal elsewhere entirely.

All but Gair.

He gave her a dark glance and then settled back into the chair he had formerly occupied—at the very mid-point between her and the six knights as if to show her, he had no fear of being near her. Or was it merely to taunt her with his presence?

But why?

Was he going to spring at her and hurt her again?

She found her fingers going to the sore lump on her head beneath the string of tiny pearls. He had nearly killed her once. Could Henry really promise to keep her safe?

"A lass as bonny as yourself should no' wear a frown." Henry said, tearing off a piece of the fine bread and dipping into his wine goblet. "You are a guest here. You have naught to fear from any man, be he Templar or no."

She was startled that he answered her unspoken question. Was he in league with these men, did he possess powers? Rich liquid stained the whiteness of the bread he dipped, and Heather was put in mind of blood soaking fine pale cloth. The Templar robes were white with the blood red cross. A terrible shudder passed through her body. Even though Henry's words seemed sincere, promising she would be well treated, could she trust him?

Or the brute Gair?

"So I may leave when I wish?" She asked.

Janet and Henry exchanged a glance full of meaning. Then Henry's wife lowered her eyes again and he said, "Nay, lass you canna leave. At least not yet."

"Then I am no guest, but a prisoner here in this fine hall."

Henry's eyes flashed in anger but the arrival of great platters of boar, fowl and stag brought to the center of the table stayed his answer. Loaves of warm, soft bread and additional ewers of red wine followed. She had never seen so much bounty; her usual meal consisted of leek soup or mushrooms in broth and an occasional crust of bread when she could afford to buy one from Angus. Heather stared at the endless selection while her nostrils flared at the wondrous odors.

"Is the food not to your liking?" Janet asked.

"I'm sure this fine fare 'twill not sour in my belly." Heather spoke sharp to cover her awe. She tore off a piece of bread and placed some roasted boar meat upon it.

"You must ha' wine to build yer blood and keep your strength." Henry said and poured her a full measure into a heavy metal cup.

"Aye, you must keep up your strength, for wielding the sharp edge of your tongue must be exhausting." Gair glared at her. "I'm certain your manners would be a fine credit to those who reared you."

Heat flooded her cheeks and she wished she could sink into the stone floor. For Gair spoke truly. Gran would have been fashed by Heather's lack of manners and rude actions. 'Twas not Henry who had brought her here and yet he and Janet had treated her well.

"Heather you look fine in that gown. I knew you would." Janet smiled and it was evident she was doing her best lighten the mood. Heather was shamed even more by the gracious lady's forgiving attitude.

"After we sup, if you are not fatigued we will try some more gowns to see if they fit or need to be altered a bit. I hope while you are here you will keep me company. Though your manner of arrival was somewhat unorthodox, you do honor us with your presence. More so than you ken." Janet said sincerely.

Heather swallowed hard. She would no longer abraid them with her sharp tongue but Janet's words cut her deep, as she realized she had nothing of her own. Her clothes were gone. All her bits, though simple and spare, were in the empty cottage on Ard Na Said, left to thieves and wild things.

For as long as she was here, she would eat what they served, wear what they asked and do whatever they bid. But she would never delude herself to think she was anything other than a prisoner, or who she had to thank for her captivity. And at the first opportunity she was going to get away.

Gair saw the color rise in the lass's face and he read her thoughts as clearly as he could decipher one of Henry's old maps. Janet and Henry had not meant their words to galvanize Heather to action but they had prodded the doe-eyed lass like the point of a dirk in her ribs.

She was planning and plotting, he could see it in her face and the way her knuckles tightened on the stem of the goblet. She would be slippery as an eel, looking for a way to leave the castle. He tipped up his cup and drained the wine in one loud gulp.

There was no reason for it, and if anyone mentioned it, he would have soundly denied it, but he felt responsible for her unhappy look and the way her light brown eyes had dulled like a wild thing that has been caged.

Maybe he should've simply left her there crumpled and bleeding on her own floor. Maybe he shouldn't have picked her up, tended her bloodied head and carried her in his arms back the whole long way to Edinburgh. Maybe he shouldn't have ridden through the night with her in his lap.

Maybe...The rest of the meal was uneventful. Stories were shared, Janet did her best to include Heather in the conversation, and bit by bit, the high color of anger left her cheeks. Several ewers of wine were emptied and Heather even smiled weakly at Henry's frequent jests.

Gair remained silent and observed everyone at table. He tried to read the mood of the Templars. They were under Henry's command—to a point—just as a lion is under control so long as the lock on his cage door holds fast. But Gair did not fool himself to think they were rendered tame, for they were still possessed of both claw and fang. If they perceived Heather as a threat, their response would be swift and lethal.

"Laird Henri?" Guiy spoke loudly ripping Gair's thoughts from his melancholy worries. "With your permission we would like to retire to our prayers. We have much to ask God this night."

At that moment, a sound of alarm and the thud of boots on the stone floor drew all their attention to the arched doorway that led to the massive outer door. A young lad with a shock of flaxen hair rushed in. He went down on one knee before Henry.

"My laird."

"Rise and tell me what has brought you here in such haste."

"We have found the body of a black-robed monk. He carries the mark of the Papal assassins."

"The crossed dagger and the rood?"

"Aye, just here." The lad touched his chest where his heart beat.

"How did he die?" Henry slid an inquiring glance toward the Templar knights.

"A knife wound in the throat ended his life. Something had been ripped from 'round his neck—a chain I'd wager from the mark it left."

"'Tis a great pity, *mon ami*, that no man among us

may take ze credit for ending ze assassin's life." Guiy said.

"Who did slay him?" Henry asked.

"We know not, my laird. None of Rosslyn held the blade."

"Double the guard at every level. Triple the men at the mouth of the caves and at the falls. Make sure the horses are enclosed in the bottom bailey." Henry barked orders as he hurried across the great hall with Templar knights and his lady-wife in his wake.

"*Mon Dieu*, Gair, you have brought this threat among us." Guiy halted long enough to point a long accusing finger at Heather. "They now know where we bide. It will not be long before another comes."

"I have no knowledge of this monk—" Heather began.

"Do not rail like a bairn, Guiy. You said it was only a matter of time before they found us." Gair snapped and stepped between the Frenchman and the lass. "Instead of moaning about the inevitable, you need to ask who killed the monk. If the monk's murderer is not one of us—then who did the deed?"

Henry halted and turned to face them all, his eyes alight with irritation. "Nay, ye are both wrong. I care not who killed the murdering Pope's assasin, the enemy of my enemy is my friend, that is a small matter. But if we find one dead monk, how many more are still living? They are wont to run in packs like ravening wolves."

Silence was his answer. So he continued.

"I must speak with the men and find out how quickly preparations can be made to take the treasure to Orkney and beyond. For if the black-monks find us here, though the treasure be safe and Rosslyn impossible to breach, it will never leave Scotland. We will fail in our holy quest if we do not make all possible haste to leave these shores anon."

Chapter Six

Rosslyn castle was hewn from the side of the cliff, the fortified keep layered as a leek. The uppermost sections were comfortable, well appointed, a hold worthy of the Earl of Orkney. The middle levels housed guild-sanctioned workshops, including large light-bathed chambers with great open-sculpted windows whose ceilings were groined and carved, where scholars made books. Pots of ink and sheaves of vellum pages worth a sultan's ransom were bound in lovely, hand-tooled leather bindings, all constructed at the expense of Henry Sanctclaire for the purpose of filling his library and recording arcane knowledge for future generations. But the lower levels, even though high above the tree tops of the deep vale below, and many hundreds of feet beneath the comfortable apartments where Heather now resided, were secret.

Deadly secret. Right now, many master craftsmen toiled in an effort to preserve those secrets and more.

The dawn was greeted by the sound of hammers and saws. The noise rang through the middle levels of Rosslyn castle. Along with the noise of manly creation was another sound, that of the Shofar, the ram's horn being blown while ancient rituals and rites were performed. Woodcarvers, masons and master carpenters built casks, chests and coffers of all sizes. The Sanctclaire crest of the sea-serpent girded by a crown, restrained by a chain, was cut deep into the wood. Each one was a work of art but they were not being built for their beauty or for their customary purpose, but for what they would carry in their depths and hidden compartments.

Several enormous dower chests were being fitted with stout iron hinges and ornate escutcheon plates that would be locked by sturdy keys. It would take many wagons and horses to transport them all.

Henry Sanctclaire had been working toward this

purpose for years and he was not about to be thwarted because the Black Robes had found the treasure's location and some unknown assassin lurked nearby.

Not even Heather's presence would stop him. He had asked himself which was more important; the treasure or the blessed lass. The treasure was his highest priority.

"More's the pity, Gair will have to ask himself the same question." Henry said to himself. "Soon, very soon, he will have to decide where his true heart and allegiance lies."

****

Heather walked in the paved walled courtyard that extended out upon the rugged cliffside and overlooked the wild glen below. Her feet were encased in a pair of undyed kidskin slippers, her body gowned in a pale gray woolen that was warm and soft as eiderdown. Her belly was full, her hair sweet smelling. There was no wood to fetch, no fire to tend, no mushrooms to gather. She had no cares, no responsibilities.

She was miserable.

Her heart was as leaden as the sky above while she stared out over the chasm below. Water from last night's rain dripped from the leaves and darkened the tops of a grove of mighty oaks. The burble of the rushing burn called to her.

She yearned for the feel of mud between her toes and the grit of Scottish earth on her hands. Her surroundings were fit for royalty, the company the most cordial—since the Templar knights never crossed her path if they could help it—and yet she wished she were anywhere but here.

Never had she been idle or confined. Now her hands itched to be busy and she chaffed at the invisible bonds that held her. Boredom hung like a cold, heavy shroud upon her shoulders.

It was all that bedamned Templar knight's fault.

If not for Gair-the-cullion she would be free and happy. She stopped just short of cursing him—she was afraid to do that. Since she had seen the stone weep she wasn't sure if she possessed unseen powers. Mayhap the villagers had been close to the truth when they made the sign of protection after crossing her path.

"Maybe I am a witch." She said a quick prayer that

54

she wasn't, but just to be on the safe side, and not invite any misfortune on herself, she kept her tongue and her thoughts under control.

But she let her anger burn.

A tension was building within her. As if storm clouds were gathering inside her body, she felt the coming tempest of her own fury.

It frightened her. She didn't want to be responsible for Gair's utter ruin, though he did deserve some measure of retribution for hitting her.

"And how can a man with a braw and bonny form be such a blatherskite?" Heather had no liking for any man that would use his superior size and strength to cosh a lass or a bairn.

Almost as if to answer her question, the wind rose and carried strange sounds upon it. She thought she heard the dull thud of blows or maybe it was far off thunder. Whatever the sound, it appealed to the wildest part of her soul. There was a rhythm, ancient and powerful in the sounds, almost like the beat of her own heart.

Without thinking about how she would reach her destination on Ard Na Said, she turned and hurried to the wide stone stairs she knew spiraled downward. It didn't matter that she had no food and only her small dirk and the clothes on her back. She was leaving this place.

Her steps were light and fleet as she hurried toward the inner part of the keep and the great outer door.It took sometime to reach the wide, arched bridge and she was growing warm inside the wool, but she did not pause or slow down. She ran faster with the edge of the fine gown pulled up on one side lest she trip. Her own harsh breathing blended with the sound that she now recognized as hammers. It grew louder while she made her way down a rocky path, finding footholds and clinging to vines that sprouted from the granite. Lower, ever lower, running away from Rosslyn castle and away from the cold, dark eyed brute that had brought her here. She had only one thought in mind—Freedom!

****

Hassir was well hidden while he watched from his perch in a tall tree. The woman fled the fortified citadel where his enemy hid. She revealed her face like a common woman of the streets while he watched her twist and turn, seeking the cover of the forest below. He was curious about her, but it was not his way to be distracted by any odd curiosity—particularly an infidel woman. So when she disappeared into the green maze of the forest, he shifted his position and gave her no more thought. He focused back on the castle, and waited for the opportunity he knew would eventually come.

****

Heather inhaled the peaty air and rushed into the thick arms of the branches. It was wonderful here in the loamy coolness. The great oak grove was more than she had hoped for—more than she realized when staring down at it from the castle. Tall, hearty trees like this did not grow on Ard Na Said—not even in the forest of Drumsheugh were the trees this stout.

"Aye and thick clusters of mushrooms will be growing at their roots." She imagined how many coins Angus would pay her if she could gather them. The temptation to look was strong, but she had no basket in which to carry them and no pot in which to cook them. Still she couldn't leave this place without something, it wasn't her way to ignore God's bounty when she found it, so she fashioned a little pouch from one of her long, trailing sleeves and as she walked in the direction of Ard Na Said she picked up acorns.

"It would be no small thing to plant a grove of oaks on Ard Na Said for all the future sons and daughters of Scotland." She told herself as she went from tree to tree picking up acorns by the dozens.

It would be a long journey and she had naught but she knew she could find enough to eat on the way if she used her wits and her eyes and remained within the shelter of the forest beside the burn.

****

"The preparations are going well." Gair reported to Henry a short while after midday. They stood behind the crenellated wall that surrounded Rosslyn's domain. From here, Gair could see the slender, treacherous path up the cliff to the lower levels. If one knew where to look there were even hidden doors that led to tunnels that eventually entered the heart of the castle and beyond it in the deepest bowels of the rough crag. Rosslyn castle overlooked the Scottish landscape for miles. It was nearly impregnable because of this location and high vantage point.

"I am well pleased to hear it. My sleep has not been peaceful. Last night I dreamed I was caught in a flock of black crows." Henry rubbed his forehead as if the memory pained him.

"Black crows or black monks?" Gair asked.

Henry gifted him with a crooked grimace. "Just so, I wondered the same. We must move faster. The treasure will be well hidden while we move it . All but those who have reason to suspect will see only what we wish the to see, but we will still be vulnerable until we reach Orkney and the rest of my men."

"I fear we will be vulnerable until we are farther than that, my laird. I will double the watch and—" Gair frowned and looked into the gloom of the forest far, far below the castle walls.

Something was moving in the trees. He had definitely seen something moving, slowly, working its way through the tangled overgrown vale. Not toward Rosslyn, but away from the castle.

"What?" Henry put his hands on the damp, carved stone and looked down. "Do you see someone coming?"

"There by the dark cleft, near the little burn." Gair pointed. "But they are retreating, not attacking."

He saw it again. A flash of pale against the green. Nothing in nature, no animal or foul, would be so clumsy to be seen.

"Send the guard—"

"Nay, I wi' tend to it myself. For if it is the assassin then he will be looking for many men, not just one." Gair was already striding for the stone stairs with his hand on the hilt of his sword. Whoever it was had a good start on him for it would take time to negotiate the winding stair and the precarious paths. But he would reach him before he got much farther.

"Or before the black-robe has time to tell the others what he has seen."

The thought spurred Gair to greater speed. Whoever

57

was in the forest must be silenced and quickly. He did not take the time to pull on helmet or mail. He charged into the glen, branches whipping his face, vines tugging at his cross-garters and leggings as he ran. He burst into a sunlight-dappled clearing and drew his sword. The salty tang of his own blood, from one of the cuts on his cheek, ran into the corner of his mouth.

Something was moving just ahead, scaling the granite, scrabbling awkwardly with no care for the noise. This was an odd assassin indeed.

He raised the claymore, both hands on the hilt, preparing to bring it down in a lethal blow when Heather's face appeared through the veil of a blooming vine. Her eyes were round. Once again, he saw her mark him for a villain.

"So, you have come to finish what you started at my cottage? You blood-thirsty mongrel." One sleeve of her gown had been tied up at the wrist, it was misshaped and heavy.

"Will you cleave me in twain and leave my body for the wolves? Or will you toss me in a bag and sling me off yon bridge?" She gestured toward the arched stone bridge high above, her sleeve swaying.

What was she hiding in the folds of that sleeve?

Had she once again stumbled on something that she should not have seen? Surely, she had not gone to the vaults and taken anything?

A million questions raced through his mind as he aborted the killing blow. He rested the blade in the thick foliage and stared at the lass open-mouthed and silent.

What was he to do with her? What could he do with her? She was proving to be more trouble than he ever expected. The Templar knights loathed her presence. Henry Sanctclaire could keep them in check while they worked to see the treasure safe to Orkney, but what would happen after that? Would they wish to return and silence her forever?

Maybe Gair had been foolish in bringing her. Aye, that was it, he would simply turn her loose, help her find the way home and she would be safe away from here and all the danger that swirled around him. It was the coward's way, he knew, but it was one way he could fulfill his vow to the Templar and no do the lass harm either.

"You told no one you were leaving the castle?" He asked, casting a glance around to see if they were truly alone.

"Nay. Who would I tell? And what would they have said when I told them I couldn't breathe? I needed air, the woods...this." She raised her hands to indicate the fell. The lumpy sleeve swayed when she moved.

"Nobody knows you are gone? Not Lady Sanctclaire or any of her maids?"

"Only you know."

If she truly had managed to slip away without alerting anyone, it would be a small thing to see her safely out of the forest and back on the road to Edinburgh. In one brief moment, he had managed to convince himself that setting her free was the best course.

He held out his hand and said, "Come lass. Though you have little reason to believe me, you may trust me."

She stared at him for a moment and then with a sigh that was part irritation and part resignation she put her hand in his. It was small, soft and very cool. He frowned at his large battle-hardened hand next to hers, marveling at the strange sensation of holding a lass's hand. For a long time all he had caressed was the hilt of a claymore or a dirk.

He pulled her to him, helping her over a fallen log. She gave no resistance. Her small fingers curled around his hand in the same way a trusting bairn's would.

As they left the thickest growth of the oaks, he heard the unmistakable sound of an arrow sizzling through the air. He shoved her down and covered her body with his own. The cold-iron tip grazed his neck just above his shoulder, burning like fire where the metal gouged his flesh.

He had been wrong—again.

He glanced up and for one taut moment, he beheld an image from his nightmares. A man, dark skinned, in Arab's robes stared at him. He blinked and the apparition was gone. Was it ever truly there? He jerked his mind away from the spectral memory. Heather was his immediate concern, not some long ago demon. He had enemies aplenty but they were the black-robes, not some desert man that lived only in his guilty mind

She was in danger. He could not set her on the road alone. Maybe the assassin who killed the black-robed monk was after Heather. Perhaps he had not been the only man to see the stone weep. Scotland had enemies on all sides; the black-robes were only one small band. Putting her on the road home would be her death sentence. He could not do it.

"Come lass, I will keep you safe." He yanked her up into his arms before she had a mind to argue. He cradled her body against his and made for the sentry he knew was posted near the river. Just as he leaped across the trickling burn, another arrow zinged by his left ear close enough for him to feel the brush of the fletching feathers.

"I had no need to be kept safe until you came into my life. No man ever raised a hand to harm me..." She surprised him when she said, "...save you. I still have a great, aching lump on my skull."

He had it in mind to tell her what happened but the singing of arrows behind him kept his tongue behind his teeth. Like as not she wouldn't believe him anyway.

"Someone hunts you now, lass, and 'tis not me shooting arrows after you." He leaped over a small lichen covered stone, running as hard as he could, crashing through the brush, ignoring the brambles that bit into his legs below his tunic. Whatever she had in her sleeve was slapping hard against his thigh as he ran.

"Why would anyone hunt me?" She raised her head to peer over his shoulder. "I have naught to steal, now that you have taken back my wee cup. I have never done harm to anyone."

"The stone wept. I saw it. You know the legend; the truth of it was in your eyes. You ken what destiny holds for you. Perhaps that is why someone wishes you dead."

And that answer silenced them both until they reached the hidden entrance at the waterfall where Henry's guards waited. Gair shouted the signal word as he approached. Another arrow whistled by when Gair slipped behind the curtain of water. As soon as he was standing in the wet cave behind the falls, the guards moved forward. They shot arrows blindly into the forest while he hurried through the torch-lit corridor. Abruptly he placed Heather on her feet and yanked her into an alcove floored with wooden planks.

Gair grasped a rope that ran down one side of the hewn alcove. As he hauled on it, the platform rose. Hand over hand, as fast as he could he yanked on the rope. Then he made the mistake of glancing at Heather.

One single tear glistened on her cheek.

Something inside him tore apart.

He didn't care about her. He cared only that she was important to Scotland. She wasn't a beauty, she wasn't full of charm. She was a millstone around his neck. He was only doing his duty to the country he loved. No more. It could not be more.

He could never allow himself to want more because he would never forget what had happened to the last woman who was unfortunate enough to catch his notice. So he hauled on the rope and ignored her completely.

****

In the chamber where Heather paced, the tempest of her anger was growing and had been since Gair had returned her to this gilded cage. She had smashed a clay urn and would've done more damage if not for the wide-eyed maid that opened the door and looked in, her young, freckled face revealing shock and disapproval at wanton destruction of the Laird's property. Shame washed over Heather, but when the door was shut, once again the flames of rage flared anew.

Heather had taken all she would withstand. Gair had reminded her of the weeping stone and in one thing, he was correct. It was time for her to face her gift and embrace it even though she was paralyzed with fear that she might do or say the wrong thing and bring calamity to Scotland.

She was chosen, for good or ill, but God forgive her, she couldn't imagine doing anything great or bonny.

She stared out at the coming night and asked God to help her. She prayed that whatever fate had in store she would meet it with courage and determination.

****

Gair stared at the empty chair at Henry's table and wondered if the lass was ill, hurt or just too frightened and unhappy to come and sup this eve.

He shook himself, she was not a child; she was not helpless. He glanced up to find Janet Sanctclaire watching him with open curiosity. She ducked her head and toyed with the roasted duckling before her. Her unusual silence and furtive glances made him more uncomfortable than if she had questioned him openly.

Finally, he could sit no longer. He shoved back his chair and nodded at Henry. "I would take my leave if you permit."

Henry waved Gair away with barely a glance and drank deeply of his wine, obviously occupied with his own worries and thoughts. Gair started toward the outer doors which led to the chambers he shared with the Templars but something halted him. He gazed up the turnkey stairs at the opposite end of the chamber.

"Mayhap she is hungry." Janet Sanctclaire said quietly.

With a frown and a curse for his unexplained softness, Gair nodded. He went below to the kitchen and grabbed a bit of bread, some cheese and a shank of mutton. Then he filled a large drinking cup with wine and took the back way to the upper floors. Within moments, he was standing outside the studded door, arguing with himself over the fool's errand. He was shifting his burden in order to knock when the door opened and she stood staring at him.

"You again." She hissed. "No matter where I turn it is your face I see."

"Aye." He said, trying to look stern, hard and detached. Not so easy a feat, with the wine and food precariously balanced in his grip. He felt like the veriest awkward serving wench.

She glared at him, not backing up and not inviting him in. He shifted his feet and cleared his throat. When she still made no move, he held out the tray of food. She looked at it as if she had no notion of what it was or what she was expected to do with it.

"Are you no' hungry?" He finally asked.

"Nay." She still blocked his way with her slight body. He craned his neck to look beyond her, which wasn't difficult since the top of her head barely brushed his chin.

"Och, you have broken some of Henry's crockery." He

looked at the shards on the floor.

"Aye." She raised one delicate brow. "And while it was breaking, I told myself it was your head. You canna imagine the pleasure it gave me."

The vixen! He couldn't help himself. He grinned—if not outside then definitely on the inside. So the lass would like to get revenge for the imagined offense of hitting her. What other treachery was she nursing?

He moved to the left—she moved to the left. He moved to the right—she did the same. In spite of their foolish dance, he saw a pile of acorns on her narrow bed. The memory of the bulging sleeve flashed through his mind.

"Is that what was in your sleeve?" He nodded toward the pile. "Acorns? Do you have a need for acorns, lassie?"

Her face reddened a bit but her eyes snapped like a spring sky full of lightning bolts.

"And what else would I carry them in? You took me from my home with naught but the clothes on my back, which I ken were too plain and common to keep since I haven' a seen them since my bath. I have naught a basket or a pot, or a true friend in this strange place." She shoved her finger in his chest and emphasized each word with a poke. "And 'tis all thanks to you, Templar."

He backed up inches with each wee shove of her finger. This fire in her brought an answering warmth to his body. It had been so long since any lass challenged him like this.

"Fine words of thanks, those are." He feinted to the left and when she answered he darted by her, entering the room uninvited. The food, he put on a small table. The wine cup, he shoved into her hand as soon as she was upon him.

"Now eat, drink, and put a little meat on your skinny bones."

Heather's nostrils flared. She tipped the cup to her lips and drained it in one long gulp then set the cup down on the table with a bang.

"Och, if I had any notion of my power and how to use my gifts I would turn you to stone just like your cold heart."

Chapter Seven

Gair stood in the midst of sawdust and wood chips with a small drawing in his hands.

"And you can craft it thus?" Gair asked the carpenter he had woken from his makeshift bed at the far end of the workroom. Gair knew well the man had only a few hours to spare before he would begin his regular assignment of work.

The wood-wright knuckled the sleep from his eyes and yawned. "Aye, 'tis a small matter. Though twill be plain." The man rubbed his head with a work-roughened hand causing his hair to stand on end. His eyes were reddened from too little rest. "Not time enough to embellish, I fear, but I can promise it will be strong and well jointed."

Henry had them working in shifts. Still, Gair felt little or no guilt in his actions. 'Twas the right thing to do.

"The plainer the better. Make it as I have drawn and this big." Gair used his hands to measure an invisible shape. "How soon can you be finished?"

The man grinned, his face weathered as the hard wood he worked. "By nooning it shall be finished."

"And what do you require in payment for this boon?"

"That ye say my name in a special prayer when ye reach yer destination." The man said solemnly. "I have not been chosen by the master guilds to accompany ye but I send my prayers with you and what you protect."

Gair wondered how many of the workers knew exactly what they were toiling for and trying to protect. An icy finger of worry climbed up his back. Henry was correct; they had failed in keeping their actions secret. And though Gair was mired with concern over their quest he felt a strange excitement as he left the workroom and started toward the kitchen. His next task mightn't be so easily accomplished, for Henry's cook was a formidable woman with little patience for men. But Gair was a warrior. He had honed his battle skills, had learned never to accept defeat in the searing sands of the Holy Land.

The cook had no hope of prevailing against him.

****

From his perch in the top of a tree, Hassir Ibn Falad Rashid watched the approaching riders. They were still many miles from his enemy's stronghold, yet there was no doubt where they were going, for there was direction and determination in the way they rode.

The riders were all clothed in black like the man he had killed.

He scrubbed a palm down his face and shifted his position. His burnoose was damp, his flesh chilled. He did not like this place of gloom, rain and trees—everywhere one looked there were trees. They marched like warriors to the door of the castle—where he was yet to find a weakness—they filled the valleys, they blocked out the sun. Never had he seen so many trees.

He had expected to have penetrated the fortress before now. He touched the cross he had tied near his sword. Perhaps he should leave this place for a time. He could go into a village and trade the cross and chain for a horse so he would not be plagued by wet feet and a muddied hem.

By Allah, he wondered if he would ever feel dry again.

"Aye, I will do this. And I will let the riders plague my enemy for a time. I am willing to share and allow them a bit of fun. Perhaps when I return, there will be a weakness or a few dead infidels."

The desert dweller climbed down from the tree and started toward the small village. He melted into the woods without being seen.

****

Gair ran his fingers over the top of the small chest, the wood beneath his callused fingers smooth as fine cloth. The glow of polish and the swirling design of the wood grain glowing beneath the torch light. The carpenter had used all his skill to create a masterpiece worthy of a fine lady. Tiny leaves and vines curled along the top edge of the oak lid. And in the center was carved a woman's name.

65

"Heather," Gair said aloud. "You did not leave it so plain, after all."

"'Tis a fine gift, of that you may have no doubt." The carpenter made no effort to hide his pride in his work. "When a man gifts a woman it should be with a thing of beauty and function. This has both." Gair had never seen any finer joint work. The chest would last for generations.

Why would he think in those terms, he asked himself? Gair would see his vow completed and the lass safe, then he was going to disappear back into the hidden glens were he began his life. If she bore sons and daughters, it was of no consequence to him. He had no desire to sow his own seed or think of generations to come. Other men, more suitable to the task of loving a woman and rearing a family, could worry about peopling Scotland. He frowned when he gathered the chest into his hands and set off to Heather's chambers.

Heather ignored the persistent knocking at her chamber door. Though she chaffed at her confinement, she had no desire to see anyone. She had cleared away the broken potshards herself and refused to be fussed over by a serving lass that was likely higher birthed than herself. This topsy-turvy situation rubbed her raw. She was a poor lass from a mean, dark cottage and now other lassies, some older than her, certainly all fairer of face and form, did her biding without being asked.

She took no pleasure in this circumstance. Each time one bobbed a curtsey and treated her as if she were a high-born lady, her teeth grated together.

The knock came again louder.

Whichever lass it was come to see to her comfort was a stubborn one, but she wasn't going to unbar the door.

Heather crossed the spacious chamber to the arched and pierced stone window. Two layers of heavy cloth could be drawn over it but now she had them pulled back so she could stare out at the world below.

At freedom which was no longer hers.

It would be dark soon. Another night as a prisoner.

Another knock; this one harder.

"Away wi' you. I wish no bath, no wine, no coddlin'. Go away and leave me to myself."

"Heather, pray open the door." A deep rumbling reply

brought her spinning around to stare at the solid door.

It was *him*. The Templar.

"Leave me in peace." She glared at the studded oak and willed him away. But he did not heed her silent command. He never did what she wished. Evidently, her gift did not include the power to manipulate a man's mind because he put his fist to the door, rapping sharply four times.

"Lass? Open the door." His tone was more insistent.

"If I dinna open the door will you take out your sword and hack it down?" She mumbled to herself.

"Nay, but I will be forced to kick it in and then I will incur Henry's wrath for he is over-partial to his doors and such. Be kind to him lass, and let me in."

He heard her! Was the beast gifted with the hearing of a fox as well as the temperament of a wounded badger?

She rushed to the door, lifted the bar and flung it open. He stood there, looking down at her—another thing that galled. She hated that she was not taller so she could see him on the level.

In one hand, he held a cooking pot—nearly new from the look of it, well hammered and clean as a hound's tooth. Under his other arm, he carried a bonny wooden box. He walked past her as if she wasn't standing there.

"What is this?" She managed to ask. "Ye come unasked, ye enter uninvited. Have ye no manners a'tall?"

He placed the items on her narrow bed and turned. One brow was arched.

"I wi' think a lass as canny as you would know by now that I do not. I have brought you a cooking pot and a chest to carry your acorns."

Her gaze flicked from him to the things on the bed and back again. His brow was still arched and he had a strange look—half-expectant, half-unease—etched on his face.

She took an unconscious step toward the bed. They were fine gifts, finer than anything she had ever possessed. Her fingers itched to touch them, to rub her hand over the smooth polished surface of the casket, but she had her pride didn't she?

"Aye, and what about a friend?" She snapped, remembering her pleas about the lack.

"I have brought that as well, lass. I am no' great bargain, and have little skill in courtly manners or in being a confidante, but I would do my best to be a friend to you in all ways. If you wi' have me."

Damn him! Damn him for being kind to her—now, after all that he had done. Her throat burned. She had to blink because her eyes were misty.

Damn him!

She clenched her hands into fists and tried to say something but suddenly a great din of noise exploded within the castle. Horns blew, a great rattling of arms echoed up the hall.

With one short curse, Gair rushed from the room, slamming the door tight behind him.

And she was left alone with the gifts and her confused thoughts.

She moved to the bed and opened the chest. Ah, but it was fine, smooth as loomed cloth with letters cut into the top and a pretty little vine too. For the first time in her life, she mourned the fact that she couldn't read. She hesitated only a moment, she had an opportunity here and she was going to take it.

She dumped all the acorns she had gathered into the chest; they didn't even fill it a quarter of the way! She grabbed it and the pot, and the heavy cloak that Lady Sanctclaire had given her. With the hood up over her head and the items secreted in the deep folds, she rushed from the room and found her way to the alcove with the moving platform. She stepped inside and put her burdens on the floor. Then she grabbed the rope and began to pull. 'Twas not so easy as the brawny Templar had made it seem but slowly she began to move. She was going down—down to the lower chambers and a way out.

She was quitting this place. She had to leave now. For she feared if she stayed even another night she might begin to forgive the strange, tall Templar for his many sins.

Heather was unseen, unmissed as she lowered herself with the rope pulley. Her arms ached and at each level, she halted and peered down one of the corridors torch-lit. Water seeped and dripped on the rough-hewn floors and the echo of emptiness was all around her but she found none of them familiar.

Was this where Gair had brought her back into the castle? Nay. It was many levels below her chambers. She tugged on the rope and went to another level. Aye, it was this one, it must be.

She stepped off the platform and crept forward down the stone passage. The torches burned brightly, sending long shadows playing up the walls to the groined ceiling, spitting when the odd droplet came near the flame. There was no sound and even her fine slippers could be heard as she walked. The hair on her arms stood on end. The air crackled with a strange tension—an energy that swirled in the corridor and filled the silence with an eerie fullness. She had never felt anything like it. She would have turned around and gone back if not for the overwhelming need to get away, to flee, to return to Ard Na Said where she was free—where she might discover her destiny in her own time and fashion.

She came to a heavy iron clad door with a great hammered ring spiked into the center. She set her pot and chest on the cold stone floor and grasped the ring. She was startled when the door swung as if it weighed no more than a feather.

A great whoosh of sound went by her and tendrils of her hair blew as if a great gust of wind had escaped the chamber. All the air was sucked from her lungs. Spots danced in front of her eyes. She wasn't sure she could remain standing. The air shimmered but was it from the many torches in the walls or the blurriness in her eyes?

She staggered forward, putting her hand against the rough stone wall to steady herself. It was too much to comprehend. Wonder, fear, terror all mingled in her veins. She was chilled, sweaty, her stomach clenched and knotted. She gasped for air like a Salmon flopping on the shore of a loch. Her knees were weak; she couldn't swallow, tried to speak and heard no more than a croak.

Gold, more gold than she could calculate, glittered before her. More than she imagined existed in the world was fashioned into every conceivable use. Seven armed candlesticks of gold were everywhere. Stars with six points hung from chains, decorated breast plates where row upon row of precious gem shone. Ewers of gold. Plate, cups, chalices, bowls, great braziers.

All gold.

Along one wall, stacked many feet above her head were scrolls mounted on dowels with gold and fine jewels studding their ends. The smell of age and power singed her nostrils, burned her eyes, required her to knuckle them and blink.

There were coffers of chased silver. Along another wall, there were robes, woven of fine white wool with beautiful, loopy, scroll-like needle work on the hems and borders. She couldn't read but Heather knew those lovely loops were words. Some story of great consequence was contained in the hems of those robes.

The vault was massive, this cavern of riches, extending so far she could not see the end. And in the middle of it all was a chest of gold. Winged angels knelt on the top and great poles of gleaming, polished wood were held in thick gold loops on each side as if it were carried by them.

A strange hum filled the air. Nearby was the stone cup she had found only now it was held in a fine chalice of gold with ornate, filigree arched handles and a round base bristling with creamy pearls. There were roods of all sizes, one taller than two braw men, rough, the wood stained by great age and something at each arm. A crown woven of long, sharp thorns and three thick spikes, crusted in what might have been blood lay within a nest of rich velvet.

She had only begun to inventory the treasure. She touched one small flat trencher but it burned her fingers as if it had been resting in hot coals. There was so much more her eyes ached from looking at the burnished glow of glittering jewels, silver and gold.

"What have you done?" Gair's booming voice had her spinning around, her hand at her throat. "Merciful God, what have you done, Heather?"

She tried to tell him that she only wanted to be free, but she couldn't breathe, she couldn't speak. The tall knight was blurring as if he were being washed away. She couldn't see, couldn't stand. Her legs gave out. She registered the scrape of rough rock against her palm as she slumped to the floor of the cavern.

She was dying. She was dying and she knew it.

Gair rushed to her and watched Heather's eyes roll back into her head. He scooped her up before she hit the stone floor.

What was she doing here? She had seen it all. The Holy Grail, the true cross, Jesus' robes, the Ark of the Covenant, the Hebrew relics—every forbidden item that he had pledged to protect with his life. He was sworn to silence the tongue of any who threatened the secrecy of the treasure from Solomon's temple.

But of course now he wouldn't have to. For just like Rene, the old Templar, had done long ago in France, she had looked, and she had touched.

Only God in heaven could save Heather from her fate now. And once again, Gair had failed to keep a maiden safe.

****

Heather was trapped in a world of terrifying strangeness. Her head pounded and her tongue was thick. She was fevered. Her eyes burned as if she were staring into the sun. But of course it wasn't the sun, it was gold. Gold so bright and shining that it hurt to look at it. And her hand burned and stung as if honey bees had caught her in their hive.

She was afraid. She was alone.

"Cease your thrashing, lass." Gair's voice cut through the fog of illness that surrounded her. If the Templar were with her, then she wasn't alone. Somehow, it made her ache less just to know that.

"Are you thirsty, lass?"

She tried to speak but the amount of effort it took to get that one word out was too much. What had happened? Her memory was as misty as her head was thick. She remembered taking her chest of acorns and fleeing—

"My coffer?"

She must've managed to ask because from a long distance she heard Gair's deep voice.

"Aye, lass, your precious acorns are here. And your cooking pot, if you should wish to rise from your bed to boil a turnip."

She blinked. He was jesting with her. That realization was almost as soothing as the wet cloth he rubbed over her forehead. If he could find dire humor at her expense then she was not about to meet her death. She knew that much about this dour Templar knight. He would never jest with a dying woman.

It was foolish but Heather smiled in her mind and said a silent prayer of thanks that Gair the Templar, the bane of her existence, tended her. Taking such succor from his tenderness, allowing herself to let down her defenses against the strange, braw man that had turned her life upside down, was odd. Perhaps it was the fever, she told herself as she closed her eyes and tumbled into a waking dream of frightful shapes and sounds among the harsh, unrelenting glare of gold.

Gair murmured words in French and Arabic and Gaelic, anything he could think of that might sooth the lass. She was ill with fever of the brain—a fever he had seen before. When the treasure was first found Rene and several other knights who looked too long upon some of the holy relics, or who handled them without armored protection, were stricken.

And Gair remembered bitterly that none had survived.

An ice cold fist squeezed his heart at the thought. Gair could not consider the possibility. The lass was important and she must survive.

Scotland needed her. And a small voice he sought to ignore, said he needed her.An hour later, Heather was deep in a fevered sleep. She barely pulled enough breath into her lungs to cling to life. He had seen this before, the deep unnatural sleep that preceded death.

There was nothing left to do for her but pray to God that her life would be spared.

And so Gair went down on his knees beside her bed and prayed fervently to the Good Lord above that He spare Heather of Ard Na Said; for the good of all Scotland and one damned highlander that could not forgive himself for past sins.

****

Henry found Gair thus, his head bent, the lass's hand closed inside his rough hand. It was galling to be found, humbled beside the bed but he continued his prayers and acted as if Henry was not burning a hole in his back with his gaze. To be watched and heard left no him no choice

72

but to admit his fear, but of course Henry would have known whether Gair admitted it or no.Henry understood Gair, maybe more than he understood himself. Henry knew Gair carried bitter burdens of guilt because of the slaughter of women and children in the Holy Land—. Henry knew that Gair would not pray for absolution for himself, and that he longed for peace, yet expected none. Because of Guiy de Lombard's loose tongueGair's painful past had been revealed to Henry. Gair refused to speak of the events that brought him into the company of the Templar knights, but give Guiy a flagon of wine and he was happy to regal the Sanctclaire with tales of blood and death. When Gair had learned of the Frenchman's betrayal it had been all he could do to keep from killing him.

Henry sighed and Gair's thoughts returned to the present.

Fate was a strange force. One could not fight their destiny. If the lass lived, and Henry agreed with Gair that she must, she had a preordained future. The question was; was Gair fated to be a part of it? Did he want to be— or was that inviting disaster?"You have been standing here listening and watching in silence. Is there aught you wish to say?" Gair asked, laying the lass's hand gently on top of the coverlet and turning his head slightly.

"I heard all your prayers." Henry admitted. "I believe she will survive."

"Believe it or wish it?" Gair gained his feet. "None have survived so far. How was the door left unlocked and unguarded?"

Henry shrugged and shook his head. "The arrival of the Gunn clan distracted some of the younger guards. They roused all three hundred of my men-at-arms. They believed the black-robes were among us. They thought only to defend Rosslyn's outer gate and therefore protect the treasure all the better. I chided them for their carelessness." He tilted his head. "Would you ask more of me?"

"Nay, I want no man slain or severely disciplined, it is only that I–I—" Gair fumbled for words.

"Worry about the lass? Care for her welfare?"

"Aye, I care. Scotland needs her." Gair stood a little

taller and stiffer. He would sooner hack off his own arm than to admit to Henry Sanctclaire—or himself—that he cared for Heather for her own sake.

"Aye, Scotland's future is your only concern. I forgot myself." Henry looked down upon the pale lass. "She must come with us, Gair. We cannot leave her here. It is unfortunate that she must travel in this condition but she canna be left behind."

"I understand. We both took an oath. I will tend her."

"When she wakes she wi' not thank you for it."

"Aye."

"We leave at sunrise, I can wait no longer."

"She will be prepared for travel."

Chapter Eight

Gair stepped outside into the gloaming. Rosslyn was abuzz with activity as preparations were made. The mist gathered and swirled around his boots as he walked. This was a fool's errand and yet he walked with purpose and haste down the bridge and into the oak grove. He had brought a small woven basket.

He didn't understand, but for some reason acorns seemed to have great value to Heather. He didn't bother to wonder why. It was enough she cherished them. He fumbled in the thick carpet of fallen leaves and wet, rotting bark as he dug for them. One by one, he dropped them into the basket. The task was an odd one, there was no denying it but he let his mind wander while the silence of the glen enveloped him. He startled a brock, and then a stag. As he watched the animal bound away a blur of movement caught his attention. He froze, barely breathing, waiting, watching.

Had it been a man? Was he wearing desert garb?

For long minutes he waited until the sound of fowl and wind made him think his imagination had run wild. He shook himself, and told himself he had imagined it."If the lass needs acorns, then she wi' have acorns." He told the little voice in his head that laughed at his quest. How he had come down! From slaying non-believers for God and country, to picking acorns in the wood for a sharp-tongued lassie. And though he bent himself to the task, he couldn't deny he felt unseen eyes upon his back.When Gair returned to Heather's chamber there was no discernable change in her condition. He dismissed the maid that had been sitting with her and bathed her brow. Then he trickled water on her dry, cracked, fevered lips. Only when he was assured he had done all that could be done, did he fill her little coffer to the top with the acorns. Then he carefully folded and packed all the small clothes and gowns that Janet had prepared for Heather's use, including two more pair of small slippers that amazed him with their size.

Heather never stirred as he gathered her into his arms and brought her to the wagon that had been fitted to carry her to the sea. The palette of goose down and many thick, woolen blankets had been laid with care. She looked small as a bairn when he nestled her inside them and drew one up to her chin so she wouldn't chill.

"Don't die on me, lassie. Pray, don't die." He whispered into her ear before he stood and left the wagon. He drew the leathern cover down tight to keep out the mist and turned his attention to Ibn Bey. The stallion was impatient to be on the road.

"Is she changed?" Henry asked when he galloped back to check on the treasure, stashed inside wooden coffers and chests, distributed over more than three dozen wagons.

"Nay." Gair bit off the word as he mounted the horse.

"I will ask the priests to pray for her."

Gair nodded and tightened his knees. Ibn Bey broke into a trot as his iron shoes clattered over the stones of Rosslyn's bridge.

****

The Sanctclaire procession was large, well manned and bristling with armed escort. At the head of the group, Henry rode his black stallion, flanked by his favorite hunting hounds, Help and Hold. Help was the hue of old pewter, Hold the color of flax. The sleek dogs were a formidable pair, fiercely loyal and fearless in defense of Henry or in pursuit of any prey he indicated, be it two-footed or four. Together they could bring down a full-grown boar unassisted. They also could be trusted to ferret out any black robes that might be lurking along the way.

Forty wagons stretched out along the rough track, flanked by more than a hundred Sanctclaire men, as well as the Gunns from Caithness and Clyth and the Templar knights. But Gair was not among them today. He rode Ibn Bey beside the wagon carrying Heather. When he heard her whimper, he leaped from the saddle to the wagon and swung inside. At his cry, a youth too young to sport a beard ran up and tied the stallion to the back of the wagon. Gair took up vigil next to Heather's head—there were no maids or other lassies on this journey to tend her. He dribbled cold water on her cracked, dried lips and bathed her face and neck with fresh water.

And against his own will, he remembered...

Gair had joined the Scottish knights from his glen who were ripe for battle, hungry for glory and young enough to believe the lies they were told. They sailed off on crusade for all the right reasons.

Or so they thought.

What man could resist the chance to go on a Holy mission, to reclaim Jerusalem, kill non-believers and be absolved of all sins—even those yet to be committed? It was a heady thought. So he kissed his mother on the cheek, hugged his sisters, bent his knee before his laird father and rode away from the peaceful glen that had birthed him.

When he got to the desert, he found sand, blood, hypocrisy and death. Death was everywhere. Life was cheap and honor was tarnished. He lost his bloodlust, questioned his faith and then risked even his sanity in an effort to make sense of the senseless. Guiy was to tell him later that when they found him they had believed he would be best served if locked away where he could not harm himself—so complete had been his fall from grace.

The lass stirred and roused him from old, melancholy thoughts. She was pale as death yet two bright spots of color stained her gaunt cheeks. Her eyes were sunken. The fever yet raged, sapping her strength, singeing her flesh, drying up the blood in her veins.

She could not endure long.

Gair looked outside the leathern coverings of the wagon and tracked their progress. How much time had passed, he was uncertain but they were skirting the castle at Edinburgh. They would reach Abroath shortly after dark if they kept this pace. Then all they protected would be loaded onto the ships and—.

"Gair?" Heather croaked and her eyes fluttered open. "I am dying."

"Nay, lass, I dinnae want to hear such talk. You are young and strong, you wi' live." Gair lied; there was a shadow of doubt in his mind. His faith was being tested, once again. Did he have the strength of his convictions or had he truly left them in that pit in the burning desert?

He wanted to believe. He wanted to be faithful.

"What—what did I see?" Heather whispered. "In the chamber?"

Gair bathed her face in cool water and considered her question. She had seen it. There was little sense in denying the existence of the treasure. What harm could it do to tell her? If she lived or God forbid if she died, it would soon be safe beyond the reach of the corrupt kings and churchmen.

"You saw the contents of King Solomon's temple, lass. You saw the relics and treasures of Jerusalem. You saw the Holy Grail, the true cross where our savior suffered and died for our sins, and the robes that Jesus wore when he walked the shores of Galilee."

Her eyes fluttered open once again. "Tell me—tell me of Jesus."

And so he did. He told her of His life. Gair explained the embroidery on the hem of His robes, were His mother's bloodline was recorded, as all high-born Jews had kept their lineage on the hems of their robes. He explained about the grail, the nails that had pierced His flesh, and then he explained how Jesus had died for the sins of all men and women.

He explained how the first knights of the Poor Fellow Soldiers of Christ and The Temple of Solomon came to be. How they were holy warriors who did naught but protect the pilgrims on their way to the city. He explained how the humble order was housed in the stables and how they discovered they were above the very stables where Solomon's herds had been kept.

"They found old scrolls that gave them direction. And by night the knights dug—for years, using the ancient writings as their guide. By the time they found the treasure, not only gold, jewels and holy artifacts, but scrolls of ancient wisdom, some reputed to be in Jesus' own hand, they had come to realize that many in the church were corrupt. They made a pact to keep it safe from any who would use the holy treasure to wield an unstoppable power."

She stirred little as his voice droned on. Even when

his throat grew raw from talking he continued.

He told her how the original knights took the treasure to France where it stayed for many long years. And how she had become part of this mystical quest when she found the lost cup of Jesus on the wet crag of Ard Na Said.

She never whispered another question while he talked and bathed her face and neck with cool water. He didn't know if she truly understood but he told her all and left out no detail of the journey no matter how small or insignificant.

****

Somewhere in Heather's mind, she heard Gair's words and in spite of her fever and the racking pain of her body, she was mesmerized by the tale. She listened and believed and then she knew she was not going to die, for her destiny surely was bound to this quest. For ill or good, she was now part of this desperate journey to keep the relics of faith from those who sought to misuse it. Perhaps her fate had simply been to find the cup and see it brought to Rosslyn—she didn't know, but she knew for a certainty that she was not going to die.

But then in Heather's fevered thoughts she found another question swirling.

What if these Templars were just as corrupt as those they were keeping from the treasure?

What if her destiny was to see them lose control of the treasure?

What if her fate was to keep the Templar's from wielding the same power they claimed the Pope craved?

****

The wagons were heavy but Henry had taken the precaution of getting strong horses, large, gentle, gray brutes bred in France, well broke to harness and accustomed to pulling heavy loads. The group made good time and were soon well away from the bustling area around the walls of any croft or burgh. The road they took was not much traveled so Gair was surprised when they suddenly were surrounded by men wearing the tartan of clan Maule.

"What be yer destination?" A barrel-chested man with a flaming red beard barked the question. He handled his garron savagely, jerking the animal to a halt in front of Henry. The Sanctclaire men-at-arms drew swords, ready to defend their leader. Halt and Hold snapped and snarled at the man, positioning themselves a pace in front of Henry's horse.

The group rode along the line of wagons, poking at the dower chests with their swords, lifting covers, opening lids and peering inside.

Gair drew his dirk and prepared to put out the eye of any man who molested Heather's rest. The flap on the wagon was suddenly sliced, a long rent appearing in the leather. He drew his knife but the man was wary enough to stay back as he peered through the cover."Here—back here, there be a lass."

Gair leaped from the wagon to place his body between the man and the spot where Heather lay helpless as a newborn lamb.

"Who is the lass?" The Maule ghilly asked, reining his horse around.

"My betrothed." Gair said without thought or hesitation. "She is fevered."

Henry galloped back, Halt and Hold still giving escort. He raised one brow when he heard Gair's lie, but he did naught else to betray his surprise and only those who knew him well would mark the small gesture. He smiled and said, "Aye, the lass is my distant cousin."

"Cousin you say?" The Maule task man asked.

"My relation to be sure, though 'tis a tangle of cousins and weddings and would take all day to explain the connection. We are bound for Orkney where they will be wed with the proper ceremony due a lass of her import and position."

"So, these wagons be loaded with marriage goods?" The man's eyes flicked over the long line of wagons and men. Plain gray tunics covered the Templar knight's distinctive white tunics emblazoned with the crimson crusader's cross. Nothing betrayed their identity or, they hoped, their purpose.

"Aye, she is a noble lass of no small consequence to Scotland." Henry said truthfully.

"Och, and who is he—this man who is betrothed to your cousin?" The Maule ghilly jabbed his claymore in

Gair's direction.

"Gair of Sutherland."

Gair was from an old and noble clan—each generation served the ruling monarch in one capacity or another and their place was well known throughout the glens and highlands.

"A proud, strong clan." The man seemed to be mildly impressed by the clan's ties and connections. After some long moments, the Maule man smiled and said, "We thought you to be other than good Scotsmen on an honorable quest. Do us the honor of allowing us to escort you across our lands."

"You are very kind." Henry accepted graciously. "Send my regards to your laird and tell him he will always be welcome at Rosslyn, the Sanctclaire hold."

The Maul task man nodded toward a small, bent man who had made his way to the front of the throng. "We have with us a devout man from Ireland, Father MacKee. Perhaps he could say a blessing over your ailing cousin and restore her to health."

A wizened man of indeterminate age hobbled forward. His feet were raw, his face weather beaten, but his smile was beatific.

"God's blessing on you all." He raised the knobby, black staff he used to steady his steps.

"Father, do you walk?" Henry asked. "I'm certain a horse or a place in a wagon could be found for you."

"You are kind but am I not on a holy pilgrimage to follow the steps of St. Kessog himself? And if my feet bleed, did not his feet bleed as well?"

"It would by my pleasure to see you well mounted to complete your pilgrimage in comfort and speed." Henry offered again.

The Maule man shook his shaggy head from side to said and said, "Och but the holy man will no' ride, but I would ask the Laird of the Sanctclaire's to see him safely transported to his final destination."

"'Twould be my honor." Henry agreed. "'Tis not far to the next burgh."

"And isn't God smiling on me this day for I am bound not for the next nearby burgh but for your own lovely isle of Orkney." Father MacKee chuckled, his eyes crinkling nearly shut and so he did not see the way Henry's eyes hardened or how his hand clasped the hilt of his sword.

****

Hassir rode out of the city walls and pointed the animal's head toward Rosslyn. He had traded the pearl studded cross for a fat pouch of coins and a horse that was not too unworthy. Ah, well, the horse could not blamed for being what it was. This must be how Allah intended for him to return to the fortified castle where his enemy was hiding. He used every tree, bush and gorge to hide his presence, only slightly impressed by the nimble feet of the horse. He was taken by surprise when he saw the caravan traveling the road in plain sight.

There was no sand, of course, no camels and no robed riders on fine, swift desert bred horses, but it was a caravan nonetheless—and any desert born man would know it for what it was.

"Well guarded." Hassir said to himself. "Much like a Sultan's treasure caravan that would transport his wives, concubines and favorite jewels."

While he watched the wagon wheels turn, he wondered what they carried, but his curiosity died a borning when he saw the stallion. The pride of the desert was tied to the rear of a wagon like a common cart donkey! By Allah, it was an insult that could not be overlooked.

So his enemy was part of the caravan—but why did he not ride the stallion? It was not like the warrior to travel in wagon like an old woman—this he had learned about his enemy though the long years of hunting the murderer of maidens.

"He is becoming weak." Hassir's hand tightened around the hilt of his knife. "I will sneak among them this night when they camp, and I will kill the knight where he sleeps."

But no. He paused and reconsidered that thought.

He would have to watch and follow, for he wanted time to do the deed right and to let the knight know who snuffed out the light of his life and why. To kill him quickly was a kindness that he would not give to the dog.

****

Gair sat beside Heather, caring for her as the wagon lumbered over the rough road. He had no notion of what demon had possessed him. It was as if some evil djinn of desert lore had taken control of his tongue. The lie about Heather had slipped out—without his even knowing what he was saying.

Betrothed! Him! The man who could not even keep a lass safe! He told them he was betrothed to Heather of Ard Na Said.

What foolishness.

He wasn't a man who could expect to have wife, kith and kin. A maid deserved a man who could give his devotion and affection, a man who could lay down his head at night without being visited by dreams of failure.

Gair didn't have those things to give. He had lost all that and more under the blazing sun of the desert.

Still, a man could do worse than to find himself shackled to Heather. She was canny, strong and fair in her own way. She was the kind of lass that would give a man strong sons and virtuous daughters. She would labor at his side, warm his bed at night and wear well into old age.

No. That was a dream that could only live in smoke and a cup of usequebaugh.

And the sooner he stopped thinking of it the better off he would be.

****

The first rays of morning sun and the shouts of men brought Gair to his feet and his hand to his sword. He glanced down at Heather.

Her breathing was slow and even. He touched her forehead with his hand, regretting the rough callused palm that touched her smooth skin. Was she a bit cooler? Or he did he wish it so much that his hand betrayed him?

"Now didn't her fever break during the night? And haven't I offered prayers of thanks in your name?"

The strange voice brought Gair spinning around. There, huddled in the corner, looking more like a pile of rags than a man, was the little Irish priest. Gair had forgotten he was with them. He blinked at the churchman, unsure what to say or do, stunned that the man had gotten into the wagon without waking him.

"Gair, you must come." Tristan stuck his head inside the wagon's leather cover. He flicked a glance over Heather and the priest. Gair could read his thoughts and he hurried to correct them.

"He is not here to give last rites."

"Faith, no. She will not die! Her fever is gone and she will wake soon, weak and muzzy as a new born babe." Father MacKee promised.

Gair raked a gaze over the priest, not fully trusting him but deciding quickly that he could do little harm in the midst of them all. He jumped down from the slow moving wagon and joined the Templar. They walked in step, side by side. Tristan frowned. "I know your vows are not my vows and your beliefs are not my beliefs, but do you not see that you set yourself up for ruin with this lass?"

"I set myself up for nothing." Gair strode along the damp, sandy shore of Arbroath. The scent of the sea and the mist filled his nose. "I am going to keep the lass safe because it is what I must do. Beyond that there is nothing. I have known for many years that I will never be blessed with hearth and family. I am not a man prone to dreams when they are fragile as mist."

"And yet the lie came so easily to your lips when you told the Maule ghilly she was betrothed to you. Was it perhaps the wish of your heart?"

Gair snorted. "Henry's craftsmen have designed secrets in the coffers and took pains to have them look like any other dower chest scattered across Scotland. I contrived to make the story more believable by providing a bride and an anxious husband-to-be. With so many chests, is it not reasonable to have a bride among us? Indeed, it is a blessing from God that Heather is with us to make our story more credible."

"A blessing from God? I wonder when you started conversing with the Almighty so that you are now able to tell what blessings He is showering among us?" With that last barb, Tristan strode on leaving Gair to mull over his own thoughts.

While he walked along the shore, where the transfer

of the hidden treasure from the wagons to the holds of the half-dozen waiting ships was taking place, a cold void opened inside Gair. He wished with all his heart that he could fill it—but he wasn't sure what could remedy the loneliness in his soul.

****

Heather was caught in a thick mist that cloyed around her ankles and swirled around her body. Her heart pounded with fear and she ran, blindly, and without direction, into the thick vapor, but instead of finding safety the choking sense of danger increased.

There was dread all around her.

No matter which way she turned the invisible specter of peril was just a step behind her.

Then suddenly the terror was gone, banished by a tall, broad-shouldered silhouette. Slowly a breeze lifted the fog, swirling it away until she could see it was a knight with hard eyes, callused hands who never smiled, never laughed.

It was Gair. He had a strangely gentle touch.

Gair had saved her, brought her through the long corridor of illness and near death by his care and his unflagging attention. Even in the grip of fever, she had been aware of his presence. Even when the priest came to pray over her one last time, she was sure, Gair had not abandoned her. While she fought the illness, she knew it was his hand that held her own, bathed her face and brought a cup of cool water to her lips.

It was his voice that kept her clinging to this earth instead of giving up and simply letting go of life.

When she fought off the grip of the dream to open her eyes, she was a different lass. She was not afraid. Facing her own end had burned that from her heart. Now she felt strong, determined to take control of her life and do her duty to Scotland.

No matter where that duty might lay.

She rose from her pallet weak from the fever but empowered with a strange strength of will, though she was disoriented and unsure of where she was. The wood beneath her feet swayed and rolled. She had never sailed but some instinct told her that she was on board a ship and the motion was the craft making its way through

rough seas. She took stock of her surroundings.

There was a hanging lamp above a small table with a wooden lip, a glass flask with a large bottom stayed secure on that table no matter how the ship tossed. She poured the liquid, which turned out to be wine, into a cup and sipped it. At first, her stomach rebelled but she clenched her jaw, closed her eyes and slowly, bit by bit her stomach settled and the wine fortified her.

Within moments, she found her legs steadier. A bit after that, she was able to leave the cabin, climb the ladder and emerge into the cool, salty air. Dampened by a cool mist—much like her dream.

She saw no man but heard the dull rumble of voices nearby. Were they friend or foe?

The ship was huge, with great masts jutting up like tall Caledonian pines. The sails were full, propelling the craft to some unknown destination. The breeze had the nip of the north within it. The wind eased and when it came again, the sail snapped. She tipped her head back and stared up at it. In the middle of the largest sail was the head of a water dragon with the Sanctclaire crown around his neck.

"The Sanctclaire devise." A frisson of relief went through her. So she was on one of Henry's ships—but where were they bound?

The mist shifted and she saw more tall masts with full sails. With each new gust, another ship was revealed in the thinning mist. She counted no less than the fingers of both her hands— a small fleet, traveling within sight of each other.

Every ship carried a distinctive crest like Laird Henry's. She studied them one by one. Many of the crests bore axes, trowels and other tools she could not ken.

"Och, of course they would need a fleet to carry all the treasure." She mused.

At that moment, she heard the baying of hounds and the click of claws on the damp deck. Furious barks and then two giant dogs emerged from the mist. She held up her hand to shield her face and braced herself to be hit.

"Halt! Hold!" It was Gair's voice. She turned toward the sound and felt a strange quickening of her pulse. She was confused. She didn't even like him most of the time but now in the fog she couldn't deny that she felt a hot lick of interest. She turned away as if not seeing him would change what she felt. "Do not speak of the treasure, lass." Gair was right behind her. She could feel the heat of his body and his warm breath along the nape of her neck. "You have seen something only a handful alive even know exist. You must not talk about it, for it could mean your destruction."

She turned to him and looked up into his face. It was stern, uncompromising and bold, but there was something in his dark brown eyes Heather could not read. The memory of his hand on the hilt of his dirk in Ard Na Said kept her wary. The memory of his hand on her fevered brow kept her intrigued.

"To what end do you protect it?"

He studied her face and she grew warm beneath his scrutiny. An unfamiliar ache began in the pit of her stomach.

Finally, he said, "We do not wish to see the holy relics used to gain power on earth."

She couldn't think clearly with his stead gaze upon her so she turned back to the sea. "Tell me the meaning of the crest on yon sails?"

"They are the arms of the master guilds." He raised his arm and pointed, the action brought a whiff of his manly scent to her nostrils. It was a mingling of soap, horse and leather—the scent of a warrior—and a man. The realization of how close he stood made her thighs tremble.

"That one there with the single ax is the ship of the carpenters of Bayonne. The mallet above the ax on the sail of the tidy black ship is the crest of the carpenters of Angers."

"And the trowels on either side of the ladder?"

"Tillers of Paris."

"And the engrailed lines side by side?" she struggled to keep her own mind on something besides Gair. For with each breath, she took him in and her body responded in strange and powerful answer. She dared not let him know what she was feeling.

"Joiners of Amiens. Each guild has a crest. Each guild has sent their best craftsmen to aid in keeping the treasure safe—forever."

"And what guild is identified by the snake being held by the measure, the square and the tool?"

"That is the proudest guild of all—the Masons of Beaulieu."

"And what is the meaning of the six pointed star?"

"That ship carries the most holy of the treasures and the Levite priests who know how to handle the relics. They have the knowledge of ancient ceremony and how to properly use the ewers, bowls and candlesticks. We pray God will grant us his blessing once we reach our destination."

Gair lowered his hand and grasped the railing on either side of her body. Now he cradled her between his two arms while she stared out at the sea. She felt small, protected—vulnerable yet in a way that had naught to do with fearing what he might do to her. They stood in companionable silence, swaying slightly with the movement of the ship, watching the white capes cleaved by the wooden hulls of the other ships.

"What direction do we sail?"

"North."

North, to what, Heather did not know.

****

Hassir stood on the shore and watched his quarry slipping away. The ships had been loaded with heavy wooden chests but there were too many armed, alert men to allow him to sneak aboard. He paced back and forth on the shore, flinging curses at them all. He wished to follow but Allah in his wisdom had thwarted him.

"I am not a fish by Allah. I hate the sea. But I pray our most merciful and benevolent one that you will find another way for me to capture my quarry."

All he could do was stand on the shore, the gentle waves lapping up to leave salt-water stains on his boots while the masts grew smaller and smaller until he couldn't see them at all.

Chapter Nine

"'Tis true, Saint Kessog came to the isle long before Andrew. He was Scotland's first Patron Saint. I tell you true the holy man's name was used in battle cry throughout Scotland. He went to our Lord on March the tenth, five hundred and sixty. Martyred in South Perthshire." Father MacKee raised a hoary brow and bit off a mouthful of bread.

"Perthshire seems an odd wee place to be martyred." Heather said before thinking.

"What? Oh! And faith haven't I thought the same thing meself more than once, I ask you? I determined that I should walk in his footsteps before I join the Lord, if He is willing to have me. And I praise God I will be able to see the Orphir Chapel on Orkney. 'Tis long been a dream of mine." Father MacKee chuckled. Two spots of pink bloomed on his gaunt cheeks as he crossed himself with two bony fingers.

Heather couldn't help but laugh with him as they took air on the deck. No matter the weather, or how the ship tossed, he was cheerful. She spent much time in his company and the more she listened to him the more her questions grew. For if he was the type of man Gair and Sir Henry were determined to keep from the treasure then perhaps their quest was not as righteous as they would like her to believe.

She had not forgotten that Gair had struck her down and that niggling memory kept her wary and distrustful even though her traitorous body reacted to him in a quite a different fashion.

She and the Irish priest were breaking their fast below decks. Above, mist clung to the ships. It was as if God Himself wanted no man to lay eyes on the fleet for they sailed in thick fog all the time.

There was a quick knock on the door before it opened. "We should soon be in sight of Orkney." Gair's hard, brown eyes slid over the priest and settled on her with a strange, hot burn. He seemed more distant and reserved—in fact, it was almost as if she had offended him in some way. The man was impossible to read and yet she couldn't put him out of her mind. She had chided herself a hundred times for reacting to him as she did, but no matter what her mind said, her body did as it wished.

Even now, her gaze skipped over him, noticing the small scar near one eyebrow, the puckered skin on one knuckle, the thick corded muscles in his forearms that made her skin itch with hunger to be held in those strong arms. It was unseemly but there it was—she couldn't keep her eyes off him or her thoughts from racing along.

"I have come to tell you that we will be at Henry's isle in a nonce. The landing may be rough thanks to the high seas. I would see you remain below where you may bide in comfort." Gair's voice sounded harsh and commanding to his own ears. It was all he could do to keep from locking her in a cabin where he knew she was safe. It was eating him alive—the compulsion to keep her from harm—and the hunger for her company. Last eve he had dreamed, but for the first time in yearsit was not of blood and sand but of Heather, soft, defiant, strong and weak. Heather in his arms, Heather riding with him on Ibn Bey. He had woken in a wet sweat with more than one of the Templar knights watching him with speculation in their eyes.

The Templars were not happy about her new friendship with the priest, who they did not trust and suspected of being a black robe spy. Gair was fairly certain Father MacKee was harmless but he could not argue that trusting followers of the Pope had proven to be a risky proposition for Templars on more than one occasion. He wasn't going to let his guard down and see Heather suffer for his inattentiveness. So whenever he was in the company of the Irish priest he was tense and watchful. He wished he could simply tell her why, but he couldn't, so he endured her look of hurt, shock and anger.

"You threaten to lock me in my cabin?"

Gair was stung by the fury in her voice. He cleared his throat and tried again but before he could get a word beyond his teeth, the priest interrupted.

"Faith, lass, you have been a good sailor, but wouldn't you be better tucked up dry and snug in a cabin? I will stay and we will trade tales of our homelands." The priest winked at Heather.

But she would have none of his honeyed words either. Her back was up now, she tilted her chin. "Nay, I wish to see this isle of Earl Henry Sanctclaire's. I may never behold Orkney again and whether the landing be rough or smooth, I will see it from the deck."

Her words chilled Gair through his padding and mail. For if things did not work out, or if there were any threat to the treasure, death might indeed be her future. He clenched his hand over the hilt of his sword, opened her door and with a flourish used his hand to indicate her way. If she were going to stand on the deck, then he would be at her side.

****

Hassir pulled his robe closed and elbowed his way through the crowd of men at the Scottish city's heart.

The hair on the back of his neck was on end, and he could feel the furtive burn of eyes on his back.

He was being followed.

Without looking back he ducked into the first doorway he encountered on the winding, dim street. He found himself in the doorway of a noisy public house where these brutish Scotsmen drank fermented grains that fouled the air and clouded their minds. Not even the damp breeze from the sea could freshen the sour stench.

This was not a place he would choose to frequent but fate had brought him here. He had learned long ago not to question fate. He found a table at the back of the room and sat down with his eyes on the door. He didn't move, barely breathed, as his hand found the knife tucked into the folds of his burnoose. Within the space of two heartbeats he saw them enter.

There were six of them. Clad in black robes with deep voluminous hoods, the glint of gold caught his eye. Each one wore a cross embedded with sapphires and pearls. Identical to the cross he had taken off the dead man.

Hassir drew out his knife. Allah would decide if his life was forfeit this day—but he would not die alone, for if these men wanted vengeance for the death of their companion, Hassir Ibn Falad Rashid would oblige them the opportunity, but he intended to take some of them with him.

****

"Glory to the Lord above, He carved this isle from solid rock." Father MacKee marveled as salt-water spray pearled in the fine white hair on his balding head. He stared up at the wet, slick, granite and basalt of Orkney's shoreline while Gair and two of the French Templars pulled on the oars.

Heather and the Irishman had been loaded into this smaller craft while the ships were being moored in a sheltered bay.

She had been stunned to silence to see at least six more ships were waiting, bobbing in the water like a flock of fat ducks. Henry Sanctclaire, Earl of Orkney, was a man of no small consequence. Once again Heather wondered if the quest was just or if the man craved more power and wealth for himself.

She studied Gair's wide back, watching the taut pull of muscle as he rowed and wondered what kind of man he truly was.

There was not a doubt in her mind that he would've killed her in a heartbeat back in Gran's black house on Ard Na Said. But since that moment he had been attentive, even careful of her safety. Even though he never smiled and the expression on his face was closer to despair than friendliness she felt as if an invisible bond had been forged between them.

What did it all mean? What kind of man could go from icy assassin to gentle protector quicker than lightning flashed?

He pulled hard on the oars to counter a deep wave and she had the almost irresistible urge to stroke her fingers along his back. His hair curled from beneath his helm and she wondered if it was soft and silky.

"Faith, 'tis a lovely place. And praise be that we have come here on the Sabbath day. After the benediction I will be on me way to Orphir Church. If our paths never cross again may ye be in heaven with the Lord an hour before the devil knows yer dead." Father MacKee was giddy with joy when his words interrupted her thoughts. "I will see ye in chapel."

Heather did not miss the abrupt stiffening of Gair's shoulders. What kind of a holy knight was he if the thought of chapel made his hackles rise? Once again she wondered what manner of man he was and how she could be having such earthy thoughts about a warrior-monk. Chiding herself and vowing she would not do so again, she concentrated on the bow of the boat as they landed.

When the little boat made land, Gair leaped out, splashing through the shallows and hauling it up on the sand. He handed Heather to the beach, trying to ignore the hot tingle of her fingers within his grasp. Her hand was smooth and cool as marble, her lips parted, a bit of moisture glistening there. He longed to lick it off, to suckle her bottom lip—He caught himself and released her hand as if it were a glowing coal.

"Enjoy Henry's hospitality, lass. Kirkwall is a fine keep and you are his most welcome guest. While you bide here you will be treated well and will be safe."

The Irish priest hiked up his long tunic, his skinny, pale ankles bony as a stork's. He waded to the beach and joined Heather. Gair shoved the bow of the boat back into the surf and vaulted into it. He would content himself tending Ibn Bey and making sure all the preparations were in order. He was weakening, losing his control. He needed to keep away from her before he lost his head completely. God knew his soul was already forfeit.

****

Hassir woke with an aching head and a churning stomach, which roiled and cramped and told him exactly where he was. The last time he was in the belly of a ship he had suffered all the pangs of hell. A man of the desert had no place upon the sea, this he knew. As his gorge rose he knew this unplanned passage would be no different than the last time, and he vowed to suffer his torment with good cheer and praise Allah's name throughout. But as his mind cleared and he focused on other things besides his disobedient gut he became aware that other parts of his body ached. His throbbing arms were above his head. He jerked his wrist but it was shackled. He tried again, the rattle of chains his only reward.

"Allah, protect me. And thanks be to you for showing

me the way to complete my task." He moaned and forced his eyes to open. "In your wisdom I see that sailing is the only way. I thank you for showing me the path. And I give thanks that you have delivered me here where I am held fast and in no danger of falling overboard."

"Ah, at last you are awake." A raspy voice said.

The dim, airless confine of the hold brought another wave of misery bubbling up inside him. But he knew Allah had wanted him to cross the sea and that his weakness would have prevented him had he been given a choice. It was good he had no choice. No matter what happened now, it was Allah's will that he should be here—wherever he was.

Hassir tried civility. "Please, to bring the key and set me free. I would be about my prayers in a more proper fashion."

"Silence, heathen. What does your kind know of prayer?" The man was no more than a shadowy silhouette. "You shall not be set free until you tell me what you know about the outlaw knights. Where were they going? Do they have the treasure that was brought from the desert? Tell me all you know about the Templarios in Scotia and perhaps I will let you go."

Hassir squinted into the darkness. "I know nothing of knights. The only thing brought from the desert that interests me is a stallion."

The shadow snorted. "A horse? You track the Templars because of a horse?"

"Not just a horse. He is from the Jedraniah Seglawi mare. He was the most precious jewel of my uncle's stable. If he cannot be returned to his homeland he shall be killed so his pure blood will not be tainted by inferior mares. I have no interest in knights or treasures."

"That is a pity. For you will hang here until you talk or are nothing but bare bones, and then we will toss you into the sea."

Hassir closed his eyes and whispered. "Enshallah." If Allah wills it.

****

Heather wore a pale brown gown with small bands of scarlet embroidery around the collar, cuffs and hem. It was the finest garment that ever caressed her skin and yet she felt inadequate in the face of Henry Sanctclaire's Orkney court.

His men, who she heard totaled more than three-hundred, wore fine tunics fashioned from scarlet cloth and over those were fine coats of black velvet.

Kirkwall, the Earl's Orkney fortress was massive, impressive and mysterious. There was a flavor from Norway and the Vikings of old that remained on the isle. Everywhere were carved heads of sea-monsters and sweeping curved arches to doorways. Heather marveled at the intricate carvings that had no beginning and no end, the representations of water dragons and war-hammers. Henry's dogs, Help and Hold, fit the surroundings as if they had leapt from the warp of the fine hunting tapestries hanging on the thick, stone walls. The pair of hunting hounds loped through the courtyard, nipping at horses, harrying young lads who were transporting goats, chicken and swine in carts. Heather could almost believe they were laughing in glee when they finally tired, with their tongues lolling out, to flop down in a shaded corner and sleep.

Everyone else remained busy. The entire isle appeared to be employed in the business of getting supplies loaded onto the ships. And though she was dressed finely, Heather felt small, insignificant. The number of people and the quality of her surroundings was breathtaking. She longed for the solitude and quiet of the crag.

She left the fortress and let her feet choose their own path. The scent of the sea was strong, the wind forceful. It was as if she drawn to someplace—or someone—though she didn't know what or who. Then she saw Gair standing at the harbor, his feet braced wide apart, the ocean breeze ruffling his wild hair and blowing his tunic tight against his mail covered chest.

He was a sight to set any lass's heart pounding. Heather savored the very look of him for she had finally admitted to her heart of hearts that she was not immune to his physical charms. But she was of two minds about Gair of Sutherland. She feared him—a little; she respected him—a little, and she trusted him almost not at all.

For though he made her imagine all manner of dark and mysterious things, she could not forget that he was deadly. Like a lovely sleeping serpent, she could appreciate the beauty of his form, but she could never forget he was possessed of poisonous fangs.

She made her waycarefully up the rocks toward him. She had grown more accustomed to the slippers that lady Janet had given her, but they were not as sure as her own bare feet, still she could not toss them off and go about like a savage while under Henry's protection. She didn't want his court to think ill of her, and him in turn, for bringing her among them.

Gair had so far not looked at her, and still she could feel the Templar's power, hot, potent and savage. He didn't even act as though he knew she was there as she scrambled the last few feet, but she knew he was aware of her presence by the sudden flare of his nostrils and the stiffening of his straight back.

Did he dislike her so much? Was the serpent now sharpening his fang to strike?

"How soon wi' we depart?" She asked without preamble walking up beside him. Since she had risen from her sick-bed she knew with some deep resolve that she was fated to go with the Templar knights, and Gair, wherever Laird Henry would take them.

She was not certain yet if her destiny was to thwart their attempt to control the treasure, or to help them in some small way to hide it, but she was sure she had some part to play in their secret journey.

Gair turned to look down at her at last. His eyes held a strange far-away moodiness in their depths, distant, unreadable, like the sea held in the grip of thick fog. Her heart did a little tumble and with some difficulty she pushed it aside and schooled her wild, primal thoughts.

"What makes you think we are leaving Orkney?" His voice was deep, soft, almost anintimate whisper that made her think of tangled bed-clothes and bare bodies. There was a restless movement in him today. His hand flexed—open, close, open, close—making her restless as well. She had the almost overwhelming urge to reach up and sweep the lock of dark hair from his wide forehead, to pull his face down near and kiss his haughty mouth until it softened and he was not haughty anymore. She fought the impulse and concentrated on the question.

"Two things make me believe we bide here for a short time only. You haven't brought Ibn Bey from the ship and Henry's men are busy loading enough swine, cows, goats and fowl onto the ships to feed many people on a long journey."

One dark brow rose over those unreadable eyes. Gair stared at her a moment then snapped his gaze away. She wanted it back; she wanted to drown in the depths of his stare. "Aye, we leave on the morrow. All haste is being taken."

"Where do we sail?" She wondered if Gair was studying the endless horizon in an effort to see their destination or was it simply that he chose not to look upon her. Aye, she knew she was plain, but she was still a lass with a lass's heart and dreams.

"We sail with the dawn but I canna tell you where we are going for we sail beyond the end of the known world."

Chapter Ten

The morning was cold, windy and gray even though the sun had risen many, many hours hence. Gair couldn't shrug off the nagging sense of doom. He had experienced the same feeling each morning the sun rose in the Holy Land, sliding over the cold gray sand to illuminate a thousand desert warriors on horseback.

But perhaps it was simply because he had slept badly—assaulted by erotic dreams of a brown haired lass. Never in all his life had he experienced such real, such torrid images. He had been celibate for a time without such happening, but now, as if he had been drinking the aphrodisiac favored by the desert sultans, his body burned, his blood surged, his body ached and all he could think of was Heather. As if to assure himself he was still in possession of control and ready for the day, he wrapped his fingers around the cold hilt of his claymore until the unyielding metal gouged his flesh. The pain was nothing compared to his lust but he at last could focus on something else—even though the night's dreams hovered in the back of his mind.

He sighed and tried to clear his head. All his oaths were becoming a jumble of nonsense, words and thoughts he could no longer manage. Friend and foe had blurred until he no longer knew what was expected of him as a warrior. Aye, he was prepared to fight.

But who was his enemy?

The lines of battle were not so clearly defined now. Struth, they never had been. He, like so many others, had gone to Jerusalem believing their enemies were less than men, non-believers, non-human. It had been a bitter thing to realize they were all just men, just like Gair, many better men than those who came to slay in the name of God.

That enemy was difficult to see.

And who was his enemy now?

Was it Father MacKee, the aging cleric with the quick wit and faster smile? The gentle little man had been owl-eyed when Gair had stridden into the round church of Orphir, interrupted his prayer and insisted he join them on the journey. To his credit, he had asked no questions, simply crossed himself and fell into step beside Gair, meeting Guiy, and Tristan at the boat to take him to Henry's waiting ship. Full of curious good-cheer and a faith in the Lord to keep him safe and send him where he need be, he had obeyed without question.

Or is the enemy Heather of Ard Na Said? A lass so innocent she doesn't notice that his blood burns with latent desire each time she is near—a lass he would die to protect.

Were they the enemies he had sworn to slay without mercy?

Gair scrubbed his hand down his face. He was weary. Sleep didn't come easy and when it did, there were dreams. Once it had only been nightmares of the blood stained sand.

And *her*.

"Now it is sweet Heather and yet I am still damned by them all. God mocks me, and though I deserve it, I would be free from this pain."

The old memories, among all the horrible remembrances of his time in Jerusalem withered his soul, chilled his blood and reminded him that he had no right to desire Heather.

He was blighted by his past and the lass deserved better—a better man and a better future.

****

Hassir greedily slurped at the water that was trickled into his mouth. It shamed him that he was drinking like a beast but his body's needs were strong. He had no sense of time or place. All he knew was that his wrists burned, and his belly cried for food and water.

"Eat." It was not the raspy voice he heard earlier. "I will see no man starved to death. At least not until he has a chance to unburden his soul and tell us what we need to know."

More water and then a bit of bread was shoved into his mouth. Hassir couldn't see, he was like an animal, tearing at the food with his teeth, barely chewing, swallowing the dry tasteless bread almost whole to fill the screaming pit in his belly.

He would eat and drink. And when he was strong he would find a way to get free then there would be a reckoning, if Allah willed it.

****

Heather clung to the rail and watched as the isles of Orkney slipped away, disappearing into mist. And though the days on Orkney had been golden, sunny and light, once again it seemed as if a veil of vapor sheltered the fleet which was much bigger now.

More than a dozen ships, many of them wearing the sea-serpent crest of the Sanctclaire, had joined the fleet. Heather slouched on the rail and listened to the voices carried on the sea-breeze along with the clang of bells, each one with a different sound,mounted on all the ships, male voices singing and the ever present cry of the sea-birds. She heard French, Scot's Gaelic, Lowland-English, along with melodic foreign tongues she had no ken to understand or even recognize. It struck her that Henry's quest involved men from many walks of life and many parts of the world.

"A magnificent sight, *oui?*"

She turned to find herself eye to eye with one of the Templars.

"We have not had the proper, how to say, introduction." He bent slightly at the waist and put his hand over his heart. "Guiy de Lombard."

"I ken your name. I heard it when you were accusing me of bringing the assassins to the door of Rosslyn and ruin to the Sanctclaire laird."

He shrugged and twisted his mouth—not a smile—not a grimace, something unique. "*Oui*, an unfortunate assumption. Forgive my, how you say?—my stupidity. For a moment, I forgot the *loi de guerre*, the rules of war."

"Are you at war?" Heather pulled her cloak tighter around her shoulders. Whether the ocean breeze had increased or it was only the affect of this man, she didn't know but she was suddenly cold to the depths of her soul.

"*Oui*, petite *amie*, we are at war. And the stakes are the very foundations of the world. What we guard could shake the gates of heaven and hell. But forgive, I grow maudlin. Let us pray we all have, bon voyage, the good crossing, eh?"

Then with a tight smile and another courtly bow, he turned and walked away, the cloying fog swirling across the deck wrapping around his boots, rising to cloak his departure. It was as if he had never been there at all. She could hear the hollow thud of boots on the damp wooden deck but the sound was distorted and she couldn't tell if it was Guiy leaving or someone else coming near. She glanced out at the ships but now all she could see were phantoms, ghostly bits of a mast, or a sail, and always, the hollow clang of their bells.

"Lord, please keep all aboard this ship safe. Amen." Heather prayed aloud.

Nearby, hidden by a keg of fresh water and thick coils of rope, Gair let loose the breath he had been holding and slid the dirk back into its sheath. He had been ready to spring upon Guiy and snuff out his life had he made one move to harm Heather. He had strained at every word, every gesture, some hot, wild feeling growing in his gut. He did not want to examine it too closely lest he find out it was yet another omen of his weakening. Instead, he walked with slow determined steps toward Heather letting her hear him lest he startle her.

"Take no more steps." Her voice was full of determination.

He was startled to feel the point of a needle sharp dirk in his ribs. The lass was like a kitten, soft and sweet but she had sharp claws.

"Your blade is near as quick as yer tongue, lass."

"I thought you might be the Frenchman." She said at last and removed the blade.

"I wonder if Guiy realized his life was in peril while he exchanged pleasantries." Gair was close enough that he could see her clearly, the white vapor swirling all around them, shutting out the world.

"Your brother Templar canna see what is under his long, French, nose, I dinna carve out his liver, though I could have."

Gair found himself pleasantly surprised by her bravado. "And if I had been Guiy returning did you plan to carve up my liver and push me into the sea?"

"If needs must." She raised her gown on one side and slid the dagger into a sheath attached to her slender leg. The sight of her pale, smooth flesh brought a roar to Gair's ears. The wind filling the sails was cool but he was suddenly hot, his skin itched with arousal. He fought the base urges and focused on Heather's face.

What was it about this lass, was it her eyes, her form, her heart, or the fact that destiny had chosen her? Whatever it was, something spoke to him and awakened urges that had slept for years.

"Your toilet is much changed." Gair observed with the lift of one brow as the gown fell back into place and covered her limb and the deadly dirk. "Where did you acquire the dragon's fang?"

"The Venetian pilot, Zeno. He is neither priest, Templar, nor saint. I appealed to him for my safety when first we came aboard, and he obliged. I am not so dim that I dinna ken the danger of this voyage."

A flash of that burning coal in the pit of his stomach and he could no longer deny his jealousy. He was jealous of any man that made her smile, any man that did her a kindness and gained her trust.

"The black-robes are not among us. Ye ha' naught to fear."

"Your enemies are not my enemies. I know not who is friend and who is foe."

Her words bruised Gair's pride. "Not so long ago I offered myself to you as friend—if you would have me. You did not say if you wished it or not, but your words now leave little doubt."

She studied his face for a long moment and then said, "I ken your friendship is divided, 'twas not so long ago you would have murdered me to keep your secrets, and so I must look to myself for comfort and council."

"I wi' never allow any harm to come to you, lass."

"Why?" Her eyes bored into him.

A million emotions flowed through him. Of course, the reason was because Scotland needed her. But there was more, more that bubbled just below the surface, more that he could not give voice to, more that he would never admit to himself or anyone else.

"The stone wept." He fell back on the same excuse, but now he knew it for the feeble lie it was.

"Och, the stone. Well, I wi' keep my own dagger ready in case you forget about the weeping stone."

"As if I ever could."

****

"Zeno tells me the outer Shetlands will be in sight very soon." The sun broke over the watery horizon when Henry poured wine into his cup and quaffed deeply. He broke his fast with the Templar knights.

"Where is Gair this morn?" François asked.

"He is taking the Arabian stallion for his daily turn around the ship." Tristan answered around a mouthful of hard bread.

"And our little priest?"

"The good Father MacKee and Heather eat together in her cabin. It iz dry and how you say?— they do not lack for comfort. So far the little priest has asked no questions, made no demands, but I wonder if that is because he is such a *bon homme* or if he is exactly where he wishes to be, eh?"

"Keep a weather eye on him until we know. Any other news?" "Tristan caught a glimpse of black sails at the first break of dawn." François cut a hunk of cheese from the wheel and passed it on down the board.

Gair entered the cabin at that moment, instantly alerted by François's words. None of Henry's fleet used black sails. It seemed improbable, and yet he had been plagued by the sense he was being pursued.

"Is this so?" Henry's eyes narrowed. "Why was I not told sooner?"

"I believe it was a black sail but with the fog—I am not certain." Tristan explained.

"*Oui*, my laird, it was only a glimpse. Each day it seems the sun rises and fog rolls in. Even the sharpest watch can see little."

"Which means the fog is also keeping us from being seen clearly. Double the watch. Use signals to inform the pilots of the other ships. Tell them to keep near. And, Gair, keep a sharp eye on the lass and the priest. They both seem docile as lambs but we cannot afford any surprises."

****

"I was born in Laois County, Ireland. And didn't I live all my born days in the shadow of Lea Castle? And hasn't it been the desire of my heart to see Scotland, and Orkney? But never in my wildest imaginings did I expect to see Shetland too. God's blessing on Henry Sanctclaire for making this voyage and asking me along."

"Och, is that what you are calling it? Invite you, did he? With the great brutes bristling with arms on either side of ye, I ken they gave you no choice in the matter just as Gair gave me none." Heather dared the priest to gainsay her.

Father MacKee laughed. "But don't ye see? God is moving all of us toward some destination in this life, preparing us for the next. I am an old man with few years left to do some good here on this earth but you are young, Heather, don't you wonder what your destiny holds? The Lord has brought us both here. Faith, He has something in mind, I'm thinking. I will keep praying and wait for Him to show me His will and so should you, Heather, for don't I know ye are special in some way?"

Special? She only wished that were true, because so far she had seen absolutely nothing that would make her believe the prophecy of the weeping stone had chosen right. She was still just a plain lass, only now she was a plain lass who dreamed impossible dreams and hungered for a warrior priest. If she wasn't so ashamed of her feelings, she would confess as much to Father MacKee but what kind of a harlot would he think her to be if she revealed her feelings?

And so Heather bit her tongue and waited—for what she didn't know.

****

The first storm caught them shortly after the isle of Shetland retreated into the mist. Wind howled, rain slashing the sails and deck like angry claws. The only blessing was the gale washed away the fog and they could clearly see each other, the ships floundering helplessly, but still clustered together as if they could avoid danger by remaining close.

"*Mon Dieu*! All the furies of hell are upon us." Guiy helped tether the whipping sheets and doubled the knots to hold the lines secure.

"It is an omen." Tristan shouted as he lashed a barrel of fresh water to the central mast.

"Storms are common here, 'tis no omen. Superstition is more dangerous than the weather." Zeno the Venetian held fast to the wheel, his feet braced for the next wave that crashed over him. Water sheeted off his stoic face and the muscles in his arms corded with the effort to keep the wallowing craft on course as the sun set and darkness folded over the fleet.

There were no stars in the heavens, there was only cold, biting rain and blinding flashes of lightning that crackled and burned along the white capped waves. Zeno navigated by dead reckoning. Somewhere in the darkness the sound of bells from the other ships rang with a hollow clang. Only God in Heaven knew if they were able to follow Henry's lead vessel.

"Look!" François faced the wind, his hair dripping, water sluicing over his sharp cheekbones. A flash of lightning obliged and in that blue-white moment the image burned onto Gair's brain. One of the ships leaned at a sickening angle. A great wave crashed over the bow followed by the sickening crack of a mast. For a moment, there was nothing—no sound—no movement—then the ship hauled hard and dipped even deeper into the trough of a wave.

"It will sink." Tristan said.

"Nay, it wi' no' sink this night." Gair growled and as if the Lord heard him, the thing righted itself like a cork, bobbing on the crest of the next wave.

"*Dieu*, you are right." Guiy was there beside Gair. They worked together, tying down casks, lashing loose sheets, doing whatever they could to keep the deck clear while salty waves washed over their boots again and again.

Zeno signaled to Gair, gesturing around his body.

"Rope, he wants rope!" François shouted.

Gair grabbed a coil and half running, half falling, made his way to the pilot. Between the two of them, they finally managed to secure the Venetian to the wheel. He would not leave this spot until the storm was passed.

Or the ship rested on the ocean floor.

A flash of lightning allowed them all to survey the ships that valiantly did their best to stay on course and follow the Sanctclaire flagship.

Then Gair froze in terror. There, clinging to the railing was Heather. She was in a pale gown that the wind twisted around her slim form. What was she doing above in such a blow?

"No!" His voice was lost in the shriek of the wind. His heart skipped a beat.

She is not safe, his heart screamed.

At that moment, one of the sails tore away. It ripped and fluttered in the wind, fouling in the mizzen. He looked up at the mast for only an instant before he looked back to the rail. But in that instant Heather disappeared.

He didn't hesitate. Gair grabbed one end of the nearest coil, wrapped it around his waist and knotted it twice.

Running across the deck, he caught the eye of Tristan and gestured to him.

"By all that is Holy!" Tristan gasped.

"Tie it off. Tie it off." Gair shouted as he arched his body and plunged over the railing, head first into the cold, churning ocean.

Blackness, cold and paralyzing engulfed Gair, compressed the air from his lungs and chilled his flesh. For a moment it was as if all time halted, he couldn't think, couldn't move. But a voice in his head screamed that Heather needed him. So he fought the pull of the water and pushed hard upward, breaking the surface with a sputter. He blinked away the burning salt water, though it did little good.

"Heather!" He bellowed. "Lass! Heather." He called and fought to stay on top of the waves. They were like battering rams, hitting him full on, knocking him this way and that. His heart was icy with fear.

"Where are ye, lass?" His voice barely rose above the fury of the storm.

He bobbed like a cork adrift. He didn't know if the others had been able to tie off the rope, he certainly didn't feel any resistance around his body. If they hadn't secured it then he had no hope of finding the ship in the night.

"Heather! For the love of God, lass, where are you?"

Then he saw it. Only a moment's glimpse of something pale. Just there.

He fought with all his might to reach the point but there was nothing there. He took a breath and forced himself down beneath the waves, groping, feeling...praying.

Just when despair squeezed his heart with an icy hand, his fingers closed around a slender arm. He pulled her to him with all the strength he could summon and fought his way back to the surface.

She was limp in his arms. He shook her, not knowing if she was alive or dead—refusing to even consider her death.

Then she coughed, spluttered, moaned as if in pain.

His heart stumbled. "Oh, lass." Was all he could say. Now he had her and 'twas time to see if they would live or die. With one arm, he held her tight to him as she continued to choke and spit water. The other hand he looped through the long end of the rope where it met his body and slowly—almost so slow he could scarce tell if they were moving, he began to pull them to the ship—or pull the untied end of the rope to them. In the dark, he couldn't be sure which.

He prayed the other end was held fast on the ship and not dangling in the sea with them.

The fury of the storm was relentless. For each small length of rope Gair pulled to them, he felt the slap of the water drive them back. Despair waited at the edges of his mind, but he could not give in.

He didn't care if he died, but Heather was another matter. She had to live. And so he hauled on the rope. One flick of his wrist caught a loop around his wrist and he pulled against it while he kicked. Then he did it over again, and again, and again while his leg muscles cramped and his lungs burned, but he didn't consider halting.

He had to keep Heather safe above the waves.

"*Mon Dieu*! Gair, grab my hand, *mon ami*, do you not hear?"

Gair shook his head. There was a voice...

"My hand. *Mon ami*, grab my hand!"

"Nay. Take the lass." Gair tried to lift Heather

toward the hands reaching from above. Was it angels? Aye, it must be angels come to save the heroine of Scotland. He smiled at the thought.

Her precious weight was taken from his arms. A strange calm came over him. She was safe. He could let go now. The water offered peace and if not forgiveness, then at least he had done one fine thing in his cursed life. He could simply drift away into the cold, dark sea...

Chapter Eleven

Gair's limp form lay in tangle of salt-water and seaweed on the soaked deck. Tristan roughly massaged his legs while Guiy pushed hard and rhythmically on his ribs. His lips were blue, his face ashen.

Heather stood by looking on helplessly, shivering more from fear than from the cold. She prayed until her vision shrank into a black tunnel and she slumped onto the wet deck beside the fallen knight.

And then she remembered no more...

****

Days came and went, the fog gathered and thinned. The ships floated onward, north and then westward, yet Gair had little reckoning of the days, nights or miles.

"Fight, me boyo, you must fight to live." Father MacKee trickled a mixture of strong spirits and water into Gair's mouth.

"Will he die, Father?" Heather hovered nearby. She had stood in the little priest's shadow, watching him while he employed all his skill to save Gair—who had surely snatched her from a watery death. Upon waking, she had found herself warm, dry and alive. Gair, she was told, had spewed forth saltwater and began to breathe. But when she looked upon him she found him white as death, racked with chills that did not subside no matter how they worked to warm his limbs, in a deep death-like-slumber. She and Father MacKee worked in shifts, rubbing his hard muscled legs and his arms. They heated blankets and piled them around his naked body.

Finally, his color returned.

Then the fever came.

Now he burned and spoke of the desert. His body was losing the fight to live while he rambled, roared and then as if it were ripped from the depths of his heart, he tenderly spoke a name.

"Reza. Beautiful flower of the desert!"

The sound of his voice, soft and rough sent an arrow through Heather's heart, though she denied it and fought the emotion, it was jealousy that stung her soul.

"Abadah, you slayer of maidens, I shall cut out your heart!" Gair fought unseen demons.

"And don't I know he is lost in a world of long ago?" Father MacKee said but Heather felt the pain in the here-and-now.

When had the Templar begun to matter to her? She had fought the attraction so hard only to have failed so miserably. She didn't care that he was a brute, a craven beast that had clouted her on the head.

She didn't care that he loved another.

He had stolen her heart somewhere between the crags of Ard Na Said and this moment. Perhaps it was when he found her in the sea.

"He is dying." The ragged hitch in her voice brought the little priest's head up with a snap.

"And 'tis that way with you now, is it?"

All she could do was nod. "He doesn't know. He mustn't know. He is a monk, a warrior—they shun the company of women. My feelings for him are wicked and yet, yet..."

"Have no fear of all that now. I am a good one for keeping secrets. But don't I know that a man is a man even if he has taken holy vows. We all walk different paths and sometimes those paths twist and turn and who is to say where they will lead? I will do all I can and then we will pray for him to live." He smiled and patted her hand. "Then if you have a mind to, you can tell him how you feel."

****

Gair had crossed the ocean as a Crusader, promised absolution for all his sins by the local priest who crossed him with holy water.Gair was a Crusader, not a mere man. The church blessed him and pledged paradise at the end of his bloody trail. In fact, the more blood he left in his wake, the more blessed his ascension to heaven would be.

He had no regard for desert law or tradition. He had no regard for the desert families, their honor or her ruin because of him.

Her name was Reza, youngest daughter of the Sultan of Tazir. She was vibrant, ripe, beautiful in a foreign, exotic way that Gair had never imagined. And she loved him from the moment she set eyes upon him.

And he allowed it. He found her adoring gazes and shy touches flattering. He did not encourage it, yet he certainly did not discourage her affections.

Just one of many sins.

Gair had seen too much of death and hypocrisy at the gates of Jerusalem, so he fled the city, sick of crusades, promises and blood. When he found the Sultan of Tazir, or they found him, camped at the oasis of Sybir, he was a weary warrior, disillusioned and bitter with his life. It took little encouragement to get Gair to lay down his sword, and follow them into the desert. He was more than willing to become one of them.

Only a fool would've believed it could be so easy. But then Gair counted himself the greatest fool in all of Christendom.

For a time he had known peace. The Sultan was a bluff, loud man who enjoyed his wives, his many children, and evenings spent swapping stories with Gair in his tent. They rode into the desert each day on horses from his legendary Jedraniah Seglawi mares, the finest in all the desert. Each magnificent mare of the Seglawi wore a twisted silken cord around her neck with a small leather bag that contained the horse's bloodline as far back as could be remembered. The same leathern bag adorned the neck of Ibn Bey, the stallion and pride of the people of Tazir.

To own a foal of a Seglawi blood was akin to being a king. The Sultan of Tazir was the envy of all the nomadic tribes, friend, foe and family alike.

Being the youngest, Reza was her father's favorite, and it was only fitting that she rode his favorite horse, Ibn Bey, not yet old enough to endure the weight of a man but able to carry the lovely Reza all day.

For a small march of time, Gair had felt like a king, with the adoring Reza at his side and a magnificent steed beneath him. The desert wind whispered a promise of peace, belonging and forgiveness for past transgressions.

Until the Sultan died suddenly and a nearby desert

lord, Abadah the Bold, came to rule the tribe and claim Reza as his bride.

When she was forced to become his wife, with no brother's or cousins to gainsay him, Abadah would take all the Sultan's wealth and rule the people of Tazir.

But Reza did not agree. She wanted Gair not Abadah.

The memory of that day opened Gair's old wound and he felt the pain as sharp as when it happened...

****

Hassir's lips were cracked and dry, his belly screamed with emptiness. Allah the great, the merciful, the constant, was testing him, he knew, but being a practical man he was also quite aware that he would not endure the testing much longer if he did not find a way to free himself and find food and water.

He tugged at the manacles. He was little more than bones and hide, but no matter how little food he had been given, his wrist bones were the size they were and nothing could change that.

The only thing to do was to use his wits, to deceive the infidels that held him. He smiled to himself. Allah was great, Allah was good. Allah had blessed him with a superior mind. And then the plan came to him.

"I will talk. I will tell you all I know." He cried out. He was rewarded by the sound of boots stomping down the dark wooden stairs.

Allah, the great, kind and merciful, had indeed endowed him with a quick and keen mind. His wits would unlock the shackles and his tongue would weave a lie so strong that it would serve to bind his enemies in shackles stronger than those on his wrists.

****

The rising sun illuminated the bed where Gair lay. His face was drawn, with spots of blotchy color on his gaunt cheeks.

Heather sat beside him. Father MacKee had gone to his own bed hours ago. He was probably in prayer, for he had made it plain that Gair was on the thin side of life and would only live now if the Lord willed it.

Heather had prayed, asking God for his life, begging for mercy. Begging for Gair to be granted a future.

She picked up his big, callused hand. It was hot as coals and dry as week old bread. The calluses were leeched of color and peeling in places.

Such strength, such ability was in that large hand, yet he was helpless as a newly birthed lamb from the fever that burned him from the inside out, consuming his life. From time to time, he thrashed, whipping his head from side to side.

And he talked.

About her: Reza, the woman of the desert.

Heather knew more about the woman than she wished. She knew her beauty was intoxicating, that her goodness would inspire poets and that she held all of Gair's heart.

"Abadah, do not touch her!" Gair moaned.

"Och, so there was a rival as well." Heather whispered with envy. How she longed to be a woman so beautiful that not one, but two men vied for her affection. How she envied a woman who had known him before he took vows to be a warrior-monk.

A hot sting blurred her vision. She blinked furiously. She didn't care about the woman.

She didn't.

She couldn't.

This arrogant Templar had ruined her life, forced her from her home, brought her on this miserable journey.

Saved her life.

Kept her safe.

Gave her gifts and offered her his friendship.

"Great brute. Why did you have to nearly kill yourself on my account? Have you no sense a'tall? What kind of a great fool jumps into the sea?" Hot tears stung the back of her eyes and she swiped at them impatiently and sniffed.

Gair stirred a little.

She didn't know why but she began talking to him, telling him things she could never say if he were hale and hearty. She told him of her Gran, of her loneliness, of her fear about the weeping stone's prophesy while she bathed his face with cool water.

"And don't you know how I feel about you? When you are near me, I feel a heat that coils inside my belly and threatens to consume me. I canna help that I am plain and small and that you wi' never care about me. And I don't even care if the stone's prophecy says by loving you I can no' love another."

****

Gair was standing in the hot desert sun. The wind was like dragon's breath, hot, dry and relentless. He was alone, looking for something...no, for someone.

He scanned the endless dunes, ever changing and yet not changing at all. They shifted and undulated, writhing like the back of a loch monster. He could almost feel the rise and fall of the sand like an ocean of dirt beneath him.

The wind whipped his cloak around him, restraining him, choking him. He fought at it with his hands but it did no good.

He had to find someone.

Who?

Reza. The name was whispered on the wind.

He called to her, but even as he said her name, it changed and the hot, baking desert transformed. It became cool mist, a heath scattered with green and dampened by rain swollen burns.

Heather, the fog and rain sang her name like a lovely highland tune. It was soothing, restorative.

He raised his face to the heavens to drink in that pure, sweet rainwater. The droplets trickled over his cheeks, into his mouth. Greedily he swallowed and waited for more.

He was not in the desert. He had left all that behind. There was no more sand, heat and death. He was home—in Scotland. And then, he heard a voice. It was soft, burred like his own. His heart beat a little faster and he tried to hear more, to understand what the voice was saying.

He loved the very sound of it.

Heather.

The name came to him again through the miasma of pain and illness.

Heather. The lass destined to be great. The lass destined to love only once. The lass that occupied every thought, every feeling, every desire.

How had he come to this?

Destiny claimed her. He had vowed, though temporary vows they were, to lead a different kind of life. He could not love her. He could not want her.

Their lives were fated to take different paths. And yet, in this dream of his, he could love her. In this dream, he could reach out and take hold of happiness. In this unreal place, he could pull her to him and feel the weight of her slight body, the softness of her woman's curves, taste the heat and passion of her.

So Gair surrendered to his thoughts and there she was. He could see her face, among the heather she was named for. She looked worried and that cut him to the quick.

He reached out and grasped the nape of her neck, pulling her face to his. He could smell the sweet, clean scent of her. He could feel the silkiness of her skin against his own hard, battle callused hand.

The dream was so real!

Her eyes widened. Ah, those eyes. She could slay him with one look from those doe-like eyes.

Damn his soul for the lost creature he was, he didn't care—after all 'twas only a dream and no more. He kissed her, hard at first, then tenderly, pouring out all he felt and could never say.

She was delicate and frail in his grasp. He knew he could break her like a small bird and so he forced himself to go easy, gentle, showing great restraint though his blood burned with lust and the fever that gripped him.

Heather, Heather, Heather, Heather—the name trilled through his brain like a troubadour's lay. He rubbed his palms over her face, her neck, her breasts, committing to memory every inch of her glorious body.

Heather let the cold, wet cloth fall from her hand while she melted into Gair's rough embrace and he plundered her mouth. It was like dying—it was like being reborn. This was what she had wanted, fought, feared, hoped for. It did not matter that he was ill and didn't know who he kissed, who he held.

For this moment, she was his. She was desired, wanted for herself alone, and it made her heart soar with happiness. She could even forgive his brutish treatment of her—forget that he had knocked her senseless—ignored that he had taken monk's vows, could even forget for this small pace of time that another's name was oft on his lips.

His big, rough hands caressed her neck, slid over her cheeks and held her near him. The kiss—her first kiss—was not as she expected. Of course, Heather knew she was a silly virgin who had no notion of what a kiss should or shouldn't be but in her maidenish mind she had thought it would be soft as butterflies wings.

It wasn't.

It was wild, savage, tender, heartrending. Her pulse beat fast, slowed, her heart tumbled in her breast. She wanted to be closer to him, wanted to meld her form with his. Some strange hunger gripped her as if there could be more behind the kiss, something greater, more powerful.

Whatever it was remained a mystery just outside her reach because Gair continued to kiss her at his pace and in his fashion. He showered her face with tiny, quick kisses. He bathed her neck with slow, sipping kisses. He returned to her mouth with long, deep, hungry kisses. His hot, dry hands were steady, strong and yet oddly gentle.

This was a different man than the hard-eyed lout who had hit her then brought her from Ard Na Said.

She couldn't forgive him that sin—not completely—not yet—but it no longer brought a rush of fury to her. And at this moment, her body's hunger was more important that his behavior and her fury at being treated roughly. For this moment, she was a creature of want, a lass who had a head for only one thing and whether it be sensible or foolish, she was doing her best to sate her longing with this man. Och, she would probably regret it on the morrow, most rash decisions had that consequence, but right now she simply didn't mind.

What was happening to her? Was she losing herself, dissolving into a warm puddle of raw desire?

She wasn't sure but she had no will of her own. Gair's arms were strong and steady, his lips cool, firm and experienced. He was what she wanted whether he be poison or ambrosia. He was what she longed for, and so she leaned into his arms, sighed and took all he had to offer.

If he was going to die, then let it be with her in his arms. Even if he didn't know whom he kissed, if he thought he held Reza, the woman he loved before he took a monk's celibate vows, then so be it. At least he would not die alone.

Chapter Twelve

Gair did not fully wake that day or even the next, but he was truly better. His fever broke, his breathing eased and he slowly wrenched himself free of the fever that sapped his strength. But along with the lessening of his ailment also came a lessening of his passion for Heather. She remained at his side, sleeping in short spurts, waking with a jerk and finally finding him staring at her.

The eyes that held her gaze were clear and drew her to him while she remembered his fevered kisses and questing hands. Without thought, she placed a kiss on his lips.

The sweet shock of Heather's kiss made Gair's heart trip. He dreamed of this and now here it was a reality—or was he still fevered?

"You...cared for me." He croaked, his voice rusty from disuse, his tongue thick and clumsy in his mouth.

"'Twas my duty since you sickened saving my life." Heather was embarrassed now that she faced a lucid Gair. She had let him shower her with kisses when he was not in his right mind, but now, when she looked into the depths of his eyes and saw the core of his sanity, she turned awkward as if the moments they shared had not really been his wish—as if they were part of his dreams but not his true wish.

"You are important...to Scotland. I canna let anything happen to you."

Important to Scotland. His words should have flattered her but they had the opposite affect. She was bereft, wanting something different, something more. Some utterance of his need of her, for herself, and not just because a weeping stone had declared her important to the nation. She wanted him to care about her apart from Scotland and duty and pre-destiny.

The ship swayed. She lost her balance and was nose to nose with him before she caught herself. They were frozen in time. Staring into each other's eyes.

Neither spoke. Neither moved.

She could hear the rush of her own blood in her veins; she could see his pulse thrumming in his strong neck.

"Ah, I see you are awake then. And haven't I seen heartier men than you go to their heavenly reward? Faith, but some of this hot broth will restore your strength and set you to rights." Father MacKee had a wooden bowl in one hand, the hem of his woolen garment in the other, his spindly, pale ankles showing while he tottered awkwardly toward the bed.

The moment was broken. If there had been some bond between them, now it was truly sundered.

Heather surged to her feet, her face burning with heat. She had to get away from Gair, away from the flood of confusing feelings washing through her. On one hand she wanted to touch his face, to run her palm over his dark stubble of beard. But another part of her was afraid of being rejected now that he was in his own mind. He had held and kissed her but it was not her in his mind—it was Reza—the woman that haunted his dreams. She needed to remember that—she needed to remember he cared nothing for her—that he couldn't care for her since he was a monk, he had taken vows as binding as those the little priest had uttered. She needed to cling to the anger she felt because he had bashed her on the head and dragged her from her home. She needed to fuel that fury and keep it hot so it would burn out this love she had for him—a love that was not to be.

****

Hassir finished his morning prayers but he remained on his knees, pretending to be weak and unable to gain his feet. Each day he grew stronger but he kept his vitality hidden from the infidels who shared the ship. So far he had seen no indication they doubted him; they were so focused on the ships they followed.

Following a trail he reveled in order to be set free of the shackles.

His captors wore the trappings of their religion, but Hassir marked them as hypocrites, reprobates and infidels of the worst kind. He took solace from his prayers and the unshakable faith that it was truly Allah that had guided his path and brought him among these curs.

He heard the raucous laughter, listened to their impure stories and realized they were very unlike the man he had followed over half the world.

Still, an infidel was an infidel, and the one he chased had many sins to answer for.

Days ago, the ship he was aboard had sailed beyond a cluster of islands. One of the black-robed men called them the Shetland Islands. Now only the open sea surrounded them. From first light to the last dusky rays before night folded itself over the ship, Hassir saw only the blue waves that turned nearly black when the sun hid behind a cloud. The black-robes had men high up on the masts, scanning the sea, looking, always looking.

Of course he spent as little time as possible staring out at the sea. It was a frightening expanse that turned his guts to water. He was a man of the desert. He had no fear or care for the blowing sand or the rippled dunes. But this endless sea turned him to a feeble, wailing woman.

For the first time in his thirty years he knew naked terror. It shamed him, humbled him. And he thanked Allah for giving him this new wisdom. He fought his fear with the only weapon he possessed; his faith.

One morning before his prayers, he imagined he caught a glimpse of faraway sails painted with symbols, some of which he recognized, some that looked pagan. He knew his quarry was on one of those ships. He only had to bide his time and wait until these unholy curs followed the fleet of infidel ships to land.

Then Hassir would have his revenge.

If land existed in this deep, wide world of water.

****

"Haul on that line!" The harsh voice ripped Heather from her moody thoughts. Bundled in her heavy cloak she had walked round and round the deck, breathing in the salty air, her eyes stinging from the chill wind. She had solved nothing, made no headway. Her heart was heavy with growing affection for Gair and the sickening knowledge that he loved another. And she could not forget that his monkish vows held him from them both.

This was torture. Worse than pangs of hunger, the bite of cold, or the despair of loneliness that she had learned to endure. This was a pain without beginning or end. It was a deep cut, a raw wound. Every thought of him made her heart pump hard and her eyes burn with tears that begged to be shed.

She was in love with a Templar—a holy knight who could never return her feelings because of his vows—even if another woman did not hold his heart.

It was an anguish that broke her spirit and made her low. Heather felt powerless to cast off the despair that cloaked her like fog.

****

Gair levered himself up on his elbows. "You were right little priest, the days of swilling broth has brought back some of my strength but now I need something to chew."

"So impatient! Save your strength, stay abed."

"Nay, I must be up." Along with Gair's returning vitality came many questions. The first was about Heather. The second was about Heather. The next was about...all he could think of was Heather.

He had come within a gnat's breadth of not finding her in the wild sea. Why had she been on deck during the storm? Didn't the lass have one single instinct for survival?

"*Mon Dieu*, what I would not give to see the scowl wiped from your face. It is too much, I say, having to stare at you morning, noon and night seeing nothing but a frown. What ails you today, Scotsman? Iz it not enough you have cheated death once again? Does your breed know nothing of embracing life? Take the petite one to bed and cure yourself of this melancholy." Guiy admonished as he entered the cabin.

Father MacKee blushed scarlet red and gathered the empty bowl and the hem of his robe. Then he scurried from the room muttering something about French savages and carnal sins.

"Guiy, you know nothing, you dinna ken—" Gair began, still on his elbows staring up at Guiy.

"Bah! I ken, as you say, all there is to ken. You are a man. She is a woman. What is there not to ken?" Guiy paced the cabin while Gair lay in the bunk and glared. "Ze vows I took are not ze vows you took. You *ken* this, *oui*?"

Gair frowned and thought back to the elaborate rituals of the Templar order he had first seen in the desert. While his body was still healing and while the wrenching grief tore at his soul, he had asked to join the Templar knights. They were preparing to sail to Cypress and Gair was anxious to leave behind the hateful memories of the crusade and the horror of the desert. Guiy and Tristan had argued that Gair was not ready to commit, that he needed to take temporary vows; something offered by the order of warrior knights. It had offended him at the time, but now he began to understand why they had insisted.

He didn't have the heart and soul of a celibate monk. He had mistakenly believed that part of him died in the desert but the mist of Scotland had scoured away all his grief. He had awakened inside when he breathed in the air of Scotland and looked up into the innocent eyes of Heather of Ard Na Said.

"You are in love, admit it. You love the petite, *oui*?" Guiy halted with his hand on his sword hilt.

"I dinna love her." Gair denied to both Guiy and himself. "I fear only for her safety. She is important to Scotland."

"Bah, you lie to yourself, but do not lie to me. I see what iz in your eyes. Ze petite has pierced the armor around your heart. It iz time, Gair. Ze desert woman iz dead, but you are alive. There is no shame in loving a woman who iz able to hold you in her arms. You cannot live in ze grave forever, *mon frere*."

"Even if I did love her, and I do not, she fears me." Except for the moment he wakened, and she kissed him. "She believes I hit her when I first found her—she thinks I am a craven lout with no soul, no heart and no honor. What kind of lass would want such a poxy blatherskite as that?"

"*Mon Dieu*, I am surprised the bloodline of you Scotsmen did not die out long ago. Do you have no romance in your soul? Do not be the roaring lion with the petite. Be a lamb. Do you ken?" Guiy's fingers wiggled as he gestured. "You have heard the story of the wind, *oui*?"

"No."

"Ah, well the north wind and the south wind had ze wager, *oui*? They each believed they could get the handsome *homme* to take off his shirt. He was French, of course and quite beautiful to look at—."

"Of course." Gair arched a brow at the Frenchman's high opinion of himself and his countrymen.

"So ze north wind, she blew hard, cold and fierce. Ze handsome *homme* simply pulled his shirt tighter. But ze south wind, she was smart, eh? She blew warm, gentle, a caress that heated his skin. He grew so warm—*viola*, he took off ze shirt."

"So you are telling me I need to be soft instead of forceful?"

Guiy smacked his palm to his forehead. "Ah, there iz hope yet for you, *mon frere*."

****

Gair emerged from his sickbed with the morning sun on his back. He was not as steady on his feet as he would like to be—a man needed all of his strength for the task he had chosen—but he was determined.

Guiy had given him much about which to think. During the long night, he had come to a decision. The only way he could give Heather the protection she needed was to take her to wife.

Of course, it wasn't because he was in love, nay, it was because she had to be safe and this time he would not fail in his duty.

Chapter Thirteen

Heather saw Gair coming and ducked behind a sturdy oaken cask of fresh water before he could spot her. She refused to look upon him, even though every part of her longed to go to him, to touch is face, to sweep back the wavy lock of hair from his wide forehead.

Did his unruly hair behave so when he wore his helm? Did it fall into his eyes when he was in battle? He needed a careful shearing of his locks. But that was a task left to a lad's wife, and so she turned her mind from the thought and the bitter longing it brought along with it.

Her heart asked a thousand questions about the man—the knight—the warrior-monk who had crept into her emotions, burrowed under her skin to devil her day and night with an itch she could not scratch.

He turned his head in her direction. She crouched lower, trying to hide.

It was no good. His eyes found her. Heat flooded her face.

"Heather," He spoke while he walked toward her. "Is something amiss, lass?" He looked down at her with a strange gleam in his eyes—humor mixed with something deeper she dared not speculate about.

"Amiss?" Her thoughts swirled but no quick lie came to her lips. She could not say, "Amiss, aye, 'tis amiss that I have fallen for your charms, you a warrior monk who loved and still loves a desert woman."

The sun glinted on his dark hair and highlighted the gaunt hollows created by his illness. Concern for his health twisted her heart. She rose to her feet.

"Aye, there is much amiss. You shouldn'a be here. Come, return to your bed, and I will fetch you some bread, goat cheese and wine."

It was on Gair's tongue to gainsay the lass, to tell her he had once fought for three days straight with an arrow in his forearm—that he had endured the torture of the sun, scorpions, and more, until the Templar knights found him and freed him from his sandy tomb, but at that moment, it seemed the world heaved a great sigh.

Overhead the previously full sails fluttered and with a whisper became slack. All around Henry's ship the sails of the other vessels, painted with each guild's crest, flattened. Not a breath of wind stirred. The sea was calm, flat, the color of the reflected sky. An icy finger traced a trail of unease up Heather's spine. Without thought, she came nearer to Gair, her body instinctively seeking strength and reassurance from him.

"What is happening?" Her voice was a small whisper.

"The wind has died." He gazed at the sky, frowning at the horizon.

"What does it mean?" She was fearful and didn't know why. The entire time she had been aboard the ship, the one constant had been the wind. Did it halt often? If it did not blow again would they be stranded here on this endless expanse of water? Would they drift aimlessly until they all died from hunger and thirst?

Would she forever be trapped here on these few feet of wooden deck with Gair only inches away in the flesh but miles from her in all the ways that mattered? She couldn't tolerate it. Just the thought was sucking all the air from her lungs. She gasped, struggling to breathe.

"Lass?" Gair bent slightly and touched her face with his hands. His hands...so big, rough, strong and yet capable of so much tenderness brought tears to her eyes.

"What is it, Heather? What ails ye?" He stroked her cheek, and she shivered in response. Oh, couldn't he see how it hurt? Her heart was being broken against the rock-like visage of his jaw, his wide shoulders, his vows of monk hood. Her foolish, maiden's dreams were being shattered by the odd smoky tenderness in his eyes.

She pulled away before she broke into tears.

Gair died a little inside when Heather shrank from his touch. He couldn't stand it anymore—all these misunderstandings and deceptions between them. He was going to unburden his soul and pray to God she might understand at least a little. "Lass, you have been mistaken in your mind on certain matters. It is time you heard the truth."

Her heart dropped a beat. So, the warrior-knight was going to crush her silly love completely? She knew, oh how she knew that he was not inclined to care for her—she knew he had taken vows of celibacy. She knew all this and didn't need him to tell her. His words would wound her, cut her, strip her bare until she was vulnerable and naked before him.

She could not withstand it—hearing him give voice to the sad truths she knew only too well.

She turned to leave but a strong hand restrained her. She wanted to die, she wanted to be swallowed up by the entire ocean rather than have him speak to her as if she were an imbecile, as if she did not ken the strength of his promise to the Order.

"Heather, I must tell you—."

"Nay, nay, I canna hear it." She clapped her hands over her ears but he grasped her wrists and pulled them away.

"You will listen. You must listen." Gair's heart constricted. By the Lord Almighty, he had to make her understand that he had not hurt her, would never hurt her, that he would hack off his own arm rather than see her harmed.

"Nay, do not be cruel." She whispered in a strangled voice. "I know what you will say."

"Lass—Heather, I didn't strike you."

"Nay, I don't want—what?" She relaxed her arms and let him pull them to her sides. "What do you mean you didn't strike me?"

"At your cottage—at Ard Na Said—I didn't cosh you."

His words had penetrated the cloak of misery. He was staring at her with a queer expression.

She backed up a step"The fever must have addled your wits. I know what happened at my cottage."

One side of his lips twitched. Was he about to smile? She didn't think she had ever seen him smile. No, surely she was mistaken, Gair never smiled.

"I have no' lost my wits. I didn't hit you. You were...afraid of me. You stumbled back and struck your head on your own hearthstones. I would never hit you or any lass."

Heather stared at him in disbelief. Why was he

constructing this fabric of lies? Wary suspicion swirled in her memory. She had been there. She remembered how he had approached her, dagger in hand, murder in his eyes—who could forget those eyes? She had backed up as she was doing now. Step after step, she retreated, until suddenly she tripped over coils of rope. Gair's strong arms prevented her from falling. He held her so close she could feel his warm breath on her face. And suddenly she was thrust back in time to that moment in her cold, dank cottage.

"You didn't hit me."

"Aye, tis what I said." His voice was deep, mellow and warm.

"But I—"

"I was not quick enough to prevent your fall." It was a statement of fact, but there was self-recrimination in it too. He held her still, not tight, just enough to keep her on her unsteady feet. Heather's skin itched and burned. She should say something. She should do something. She should—"Faith, but the wind has deserted us." Father MacKee appeared from nowhere. His balding head was pink, his eyes troubled as he scanned the skies. "'Tis good to see you hale and hearty and taking a turn around the ship, but I thought to find you in prayer with your brother knights."

Gair frowned and stared deep into Heather's eyes. "'Tis time I explained about that as well. I am not a Templar—not a true Templar."

Once again, she didn't know what to say—what to do. What could he mean by that? Over his long suit of chain mail, he wore the white tunic with the crimson cross. She was saved from asking him though because Father MacKee spoke.

"And if you be not a Knight of Solomon's Temple, my boy, then what exactly are you?"

Finally, Heather found some inner strength. She pushed herself free of Gair's arms, a new wave of unease folding over her. "Aye, I would ask the same thing of you, Gair. If not a warrior-monk on a holy quest, then what are you?"

****

"There is not a single breath of a breeze." Zeno, the

Venetian pilot, stood on the deck, his dark eyes trained on the vista. Henry's fleet bobbed like corks on the dead-calm ocean while a few seabirds flew overhead. "We are nearby the island where the Norsemen reside." Zeno commented.

"How much of our journey lies before us?" Gair knew the wind was fickle but every moment lost weighed heavy on him. Wariness of the little priest was still thick on the ship. Now with the lack of wind the Templar knights were edgy, pacing like caged cats, suspicion and fear seeping into the air around them.

When a glimpse of a black sail was spotted this morn, dire speculation roiled to the surface. Father MacKee was being watched, Heather was being avoided, and Gair could not help himself. He knew he was behaving like a desert lion with a thorn in his paw, but every moment they lingered, helpless and adrift undermined the quest and brought dangerous emotions to Henry's ship. Something had to be done.

He turned to Henry. "You must act, Henry. You must do as we discussed."

"Do you really believe it would make a difference, Gair?"

He nodded. "Faith is all that remains of the virtues I once held dear."

"Launch the small boat." Henry bellowed, striding across the deck. The once bright wood of his magnificent flag ship was weathering, everything becoming a hoary gray almost as if it mirrored the mood of those onboard.

Half a dozen Sanctclaire men uncoiled ropes and began to lower a small boat into the water. When it hit the placid surface with a hollow splash a ladder of rope was unfurled over the side of the ship. It dangled more than three feet above the little boat. Several burly Scot's shinnied down the ropes, dropped into it, and took up oars.

Henry swung a leg over the railing and started down the ladder, swaying slightly with each step. Gair watched him from the railing. When Henry was settled, he looked up. "While the wind is down I would visit with the Hebrew priests. We need a miracle. And we need it now."

****

Heather peered out the porthole and watched

Henry's departure. She had been so shaken by everything that had happened with Gair that she had fled, like the coward she was, to her cabin. Now she cringed in her bunk, confused, unsure, almost the same fearful lass that had first glimpsed Gair in the rain on the slopes of Ard Na Said.

"Silly little goose." She chided herself. What was happening to her? She was of two minds on every subject. She couldn't get close enough to Gair—she could not find refuge far enough away. She hated him, feared him, didn't trust him—she trusted him with her life.

"He took me from my home." And brought her on an adventure that warmed her blood and made her heart trill.

"He saved my life—more than once." She thought of his illness, how she had prayed for his salvation, touched him, reveled in the moments when he kissed her.

"I am losing my wits." She laced her fingers together to halt their trembling.

A knock at the door brought a squeak of surprise escaping from her lips. To her horror—or was it excitement?—the door opened and Gair filled the space with his wide shoulders. He ducked his head to enter the cabin, and suddenly the space was inadequate, too small, too close, filled with him and his braw aura of manhood.

"Lass?"

"Aye?"

"We dinnae finish our talk." He halted where he stood but she felt trapped, hemmed in by her own emotions and confusion.

"You have naught to say I wish to hear. Every time you speak you spin a web that only serves to confuse me." Her gaze darted around the cabin. There was only one door and Gair blocked it. He stood tall, erect, but his manner was a bit uncertain.

"You ken that you are important to Scotland?" He looked into her eyes but then his gaze slid away.

"You have told me oft enough, I should ken by now." His words stung each time he reminded that her only value to him was because of the weeping stone's prophesy.

"I thought I, that is to say, if Scotland lost you to the sea." He inched nearer, speaking low as he might to a wounded doe. "The prospect is inconceivable—for Scotland."

"You saved me—because of the prophesy. Aye, I understand." Her heart tumbled when she caught a whiff of his scent. It was a heady combination of Scot, sea, and the strange attraction she hated but was powerless to halt.

"I worry overmuch, lass, that I willna' be near when you need me—to keep you safe." His brow was furrowed. The wavy lock of hair dangling near his eyes.

Her fingers itched. She balled up her fist to deny the urges she felt.

"Do you ken, lass?" Once again, their eyes locked and then his gaze slid away.

"No." She said to her own yearnings.

"I am making a hash of what I want to say." Gair scrubbed his hand down his face. His movement brought her gaze to the bright red cross on his tunic. The symbol of how she had no hope of a life with him. Then she remembered his confusing words.

"What did you mean when you said you had taken temporary vows?"

"'Tis what I'm trying to tell you, lassie. I am no true Templar. Guiy and Tristan wouldn'a let me take the permanent vows of the Order—the vow to shun a woman's company—the vow to remain chaste...*celibate*. I am no true Templar knight—no warrior monk sworn to live alone. I have been celibate but—"

"Celibate?"

"Damn and blast, Heather, can no you no' see what I am asking?"

"You have asked me naught!" The tension in her body was making her giddy; she wanted to run, to stay. *Prithee, Lord, make him leave me in peace*! She prayed.

"Heather, I must keep you safe. You need to be near me, always, so I can keep you safe...I need to take you to wife."

He reached out, grabbed her by the arm and hauled her to him. Her heart kicked inside her breast. Then as if she were his beloved Reza, he placed his lips over hers and plundered her mouth. His kiss was hungry, tender, demanding all in one. Heather resisted for half a heartbeat, and then she wrapped her arms around his neck, feeling the silken sweep of his longish hair on the backs of her hands. She returned his kiss with all the desperate longing of a woman who loves and knows she will never be loved in return. She was hungry for what she could have in this precious march of time.

She kneaded the powerful muscles on the top of his shoulders, skimmed her palms along his jaws. The kiss deepened.

It would be good-sense on her part to pull away, to deny him—to tell him she would be no man's wife unless he loved her. She should tell him that. She knew his heart beat for a desert woman. She should do the sensible thing, but she did not.

Instead, she let her body mold itself to his, and in that moment when the deck seemed to sway beneath her feet and the sky overhead rumbled, she made a decision.

She loved him enough for both of them. She was only a poor lass from Ard Na Said who expected little from life. Maybe the stone was right, maybe it wasn't. But either way she was going to take what Gair offered.

She knew he didn't love her, knew he offered his protection only out of duty and his great love of Scotland.

But that was enough for her.

She pulled away and looked deep into his eyes. Their gaze locked and held. He did not look away. In that moment, her fate was sealed.

"Aye, Gair. I will wed you."

Chapter Fourteen

"I wi' guard you with my life. I will keep you from harm."

It was not a profession of love, but it was more than Heather ever expected to hear. It was enough, or so she told herself.

"We must tell Henry Sanctclaire. I would have the deed done with all haste." He rubbed his knuckles against her cheek as he spoke. "I want to have you with me—for your safety—as quickly as I may."

Haste, aye, Gair might not be a Templar but he held his duty and honor dear, he would want to see the deed done quickly. For Scotland. That reality pierced her, once again."He rowed to the boat with the six sided star—to the Levite priests." She was eager as well, but not for the same reason. She wanted the ceremony performed before Gair changed his mind.

"Aye, he is conferring with the Hebrew priests about the lack of wind."

Heather had it in mind to ask what he thought the Hebrews could do about the wind, when a loud commotion on deck brought Gair spinning around. He flung open her door and strode away. She scrambled after him not wishing any distance to be between them.

Laird Henry was climbing the rope ladder. A loud noise, melodic but foreign, like many voices raised in monotone song, was coming from the Hebrew ship. The Shofar was blown, the sound carrying over the waves, a deep drum was being beat. Almost in answer, the strange sound of rumbling thunder came from far over the watery horizon.

The Sanctclaire clung to the rope ladder and flung his leg over the railing. Men hauled the small boat up the side of the ship while a great shudder moved along the surface of the water. Tiny ripples appeared in the glassy surface. Then with a sigh, as if God had released a long-held breath, the wind rose. The gust strengthened and filled the billowing canvas. The deck shivered beneath Heather's feet. Then a dozen ships tilted and slowly began to cut through the growing waves.

"We have our miracle!" Henry shouted as the men fell to their tasks, taking advantage of the wind. "Zeno, point us to the ends of the earth!"

****

Hassir was at his midday prayer when he felt the movement of the ship. Allah, the merciful, had answered his fervent pleas. He put his face to the bare wood floor upon which he knelt and thanked Allah for his bountiful goodness while his mighty breath filled the black sails.

With Allah's help he would yet catch the infidel and regain the desert treasure.

****

"*Mon frere*, I am pleased to see you followed my advice. Did you drop to one knee and tell the petite that you love her?" Guiy elbowed Gair and waggled his brows at Tristan. Raymond and the other Templars were subdued. It was an unusual occurrence. Rarely had one of the Order, even one not yet bound by the last vows, returned to his former life.

"Are all Frenchmen as deaf as you? I have reasons of my own for wedding the lass, but love is not among them." Gair snapped.

The Templars exchanged glances. Some looked confused, some looked doubtful. Guiy looked doubtful and amused.

"Bah, the Lord wasted his time giving you ze *bon* body and handsome face. You have no heart, no soul. What a waste. A Frenchman would know how to employ your virtues. Myself, if I was not bound by holy vows, would show you how to make love to the petite."

Gair exploded from the bench as if loosed from a crossbow. His face was a vision of fury. "Never, ever, speak of Heather in that fashion or I will relieve you of your French tongue."

Guiy raised a brow and slouched on one elbow. "Ah, so that iz how it iz, eh? Have it your way, Gair, you do not love the petite. You marry her for reasons of your own that have nothing to do with the hot fire of jealousy coursing through your blood. At last, I understand, *oui*."

Gair clamped his lips tight and stalked away. Guiy didn't understand, damn his French hide! Heather was important...to Scotland. He didn't love her. He couldn't love her. Gair had learned that bitter lesson only too well.

But he would keep he safe.

Even from himself.

****

"If there is to be a wedding between Heather and Gair, then I will see it done." Henry told the little priest who glared defiantly at him.

"Captain of this craft you may be, but I am an ordained priest. I can give their joining the sanctification it deserves. Or do you not observe the power of Rome?"

Tension rippled through the throng that had gathered. Gair stood a small space from Heather while Templar knights, Zeno the Venetian, Scottish sailors and Sanctclaire task men looked on.

The answer to that question was on every tongue. Hands flexed at the hilt of dirk and sword while a prolonged silence followed.

Wasn't that exactly the mortise and tenon of this voyage? Henry and the Templars defied the Pope, hated his grasping ways, and had learned the hard way that his beliefs could be swayed by a determined monarch who owed too much money but possessed almost unlimited power. The French king, in debt to the Templar Order had persuaded the Pope to condemn them all to death years ago. The survivor's were now outlaw—outcast— their faith questioned and reviled.

"I shall decide." Heather broke the silence. She stepped forward. "I am the bride. I shall decide who will officiate."

All eyes swiveled to her. A sudden defiance and strength surged through her. She nodded at the priest and turned to glare at the Sanctclaire Earl.

"Lord Henry, how soon before we make landfall?" She asked, emboldened by a power that settled over her like the sea-mist.

Henry raised a brow, his lips twitched but he did not smile nor did he frown. "Our navigator tells me we should reach our destination in a fortnight...my lady."

Heather fought the heat that climbed her cheeks. "Then I would be honored if you would allow me to be wed on land."

"Faith, and isn't that a grand idea? And who will be officiating at the ceremony?" Father MacKee smiled slyly, obviously expecting her to choose him over the Earl.

"Both of you." Heather waited for Gair to gainsay her but he did not. In fact, he took a step nearer to her. She felt the stalwart bulwark of his presence and gained more strength from it. They were a unified couple—even before they were wed—at least in this. That warmed her. He might not love her, but he would respect her and do his best to support her.

Henry inclined his head. "Very well, my lady. When we land you shall be wed—in whatever design you desire."

****

The next morning Heather woke to the sound of knocking at her cabin door. She had slept in a cocoon of dreams where Gair loved her and cared for her for herself and not as the object of a weeping stone's prophecy. The noise tugged her from the lovely, sweet realm of what she wished instead of what truly existed.

When she could no longer ignore the sound, she dragged herself from the bunk and threw the latch on the door. Gair stared at her over a pile of silken cloth each fold a different colored bar of a bright rainbow.

"Morn. Lord Henry tells me a lass has need for many garments. I have no skill in these matters but the hues are pleasing to my eyes. I carried this from the East, never knowing what to do with it, but enjoying the color and the feel. Fashion it into whatever you need or want— if it is adequate for a lady's use."

Gair cleared his throat and shifted one booted foot. Heather couldn't help but smile. It was so unlike him to be unsure and apologetic. She stepped aside and he entered, forgetting to duck, soundly cracking his skull on the lintel.

The look on his face made Heather swallow a giggle. He raised a brow and his eyes crinkled as if he might smile but it died aborning on his lips. He was still the same stern man when he said, "I'm going to break my fast—," He let the words trail off.

Heather waited for him to take up the thought again but he did not. He just stood there, holding the cloth, staring at her.

What was wrong with him? Was he already regretting his proposal? Did he wish to recant and wasn't sure how to do it?

"You may leave the cloth." Her heart was aching.

He dumped it all in a heap on the bunk. Then he turned to her.

"It is strangely cool, there is need of a cloak."

"In my cabin?"

"Nay. Once again my tongue is awkward." He took in a deep breath and frowned. Was it so difficult for him to speak with her? She fought the despair that contracted her heart.

"Come above, lass. Break your fast with me, and the morning air is chilled, so you will have need of a cloak."

"So you can watch over me?" There was bitterness and hurt in her voice and she prayed he didn't notice it.

"Aye, so I can keep you safe."

She went above with Gair at her heels. Indeed the air was chilled.

The cheese was sharp with age, the wine watered, but Heather noticed little of the meal. All she could think about was Gair next to her on the splintery bench. The air was strangely crisp, almost biting with cold, but at least the wind held, filling the sails and pushing them ever westward toward an unknown destination.

Toward the day, she would wed Gair.

Toward her heart's desire and her biggest fear.

Toward whatever safe haven they had found for the secret, holy treasure.

"*Viola! Viola!*"

French voices raised in alarm brought Gair up from the bench. He sprinted to the railing.

Heather followed, emerging to find everyone on board busy while the pilot, Zeno, shouted orders and hauled on the great wheel that guided the ship.

There in their path was an enormous floating island of bluish white. Only after Heather blinked several times did she realize the island was formed completely of ice.

"Are we lost? Are we at the edge of the world?" Heather gripped the railing and stared, unable to move.

"*Non*, petite, we are not *perdu*, lost. It is the floating island of ice, *oui*?" The ship was turning slightly, the hull slipping silently by the obstacle. The uppermost part of the ice towered over the masts, dwarfing the ship, making Heather tremble beneath its shadow. A strange sound filled the air, and she realized with horror that it was wood scraping on ice. Chunks the size of the Templar shields began to rain down. Sharp shards embedded in the wood like the blade of a dirk, or the edge of an ax. She could only stare at the rime.

Halt and Hold barked furiously, snapping at chunks of ice that rained onto the deck.

"Heather!"

She turned to see Gair bearing down on her. His face was dark, his hard eyes glittering. One rock hard arm swept her from her feet. The air was forced from her lungs and they tumbled together, arms, legs and cloaks tangled into a heap against a keg. Pain shot up her arm.

"You are hurting me!" She screamed, pounding her fists ineffectually against the hard bulk of his chest.

"I am saving your life." He grated out.

He was laying on his side, looking back at the spot where moments ago she had been standing. A large block of ice had fallen onto the deck, breaking part of it away.

She turned back to Gair. Her heart was beating fast, she was shivering.

He was so close she could feel his breath, and see the flecks of gold in his dark eyes. She noticed a narrow, white, scar on his brow.

His arm around her was warm, hard, possessive.

It would only require her to lean toward him a wee bit and their lips would be touching.

Do it. Do it. Do it. Her heartbeat said.

She closed her eyes and leaned toward him...

Gair watched Heather's lashes flutter down over her eyes and his heart tumbled. Once again, he had barely managed to keep her from harm.

Was the lass forever to be in jeopardy? Or was it because of him that she was at risk? If he had left her alone on Ard Na Said she would not be here, on this ship, in this danger, sailing to an unknown land to do the impossible.

Guilt and the old sting of responsibility surged through him. He wanted her safe...that is all he wanted—to keep her safe. He couldn't love her...he couldn't kiss her, hold her, touch her.

He didn't deserve love.

Gair stood up abruptly.

Heather's eyes snapped open, shock and some other emotion he could not read widened them.

"Easy, lass." He pulled her gently to her feet. "Are you hurt? Is there anything broken?"

She jerked her arm from his grasp and sucked in a breath. "Nay, I am in one piece. You may rest easy knowing you have done your duty. I am unharmed." Then with a last glance at the ice on deck she skirted passed it and went below.

The temperature dropped right along with his heart.

Chapter Fifteen

Gair walked Ibn Bey carefully around the hole in the deck. The ship's carpenter was busy making repairs, but for the moment, it was a treacherous obstacle for delicate bones and hoof. Since Gair had risen from his sickbed, he had resumed his pattern of walking the horse before he broke his own fast. The stallion needed fresh air and exercise to remain strong and fit. Gair hadn't yet asked which of the Templars had seen to the task while he was ill, a lack he needs must remedy so that he could express his gratitude to his brother's in arms.

He rounded the forecastle when Ibn Bey's nose came up. He whinnied loud and long, the stallion calling out to his own kind.

"Ah, so you miss the company of a mare, do you?" Gair held the lead loosely in his hand. Ibn Bey remained with him out of choice more than a tight rein. The only other person to ride him had been Reza—and Heather, when he gave the horse no choice but to carry her as captive from Ard Na Said.

Ibn Bey's sides quivered as he nickered again, the shrill sound wafting over the waves. If other horses, on other ships, heard and answered, Gair didn't know. With a jerk of his head Ibn Bey half reared on his hind legs, then he lunged away from Gair who was so startled by the unusual action, he did not react quickly enough to stop him.

The horse skidded on the damp, weathered deck, nearly losing his footing, one hip dipping nearly to the deck. Then he was rushing beyond the kegs of water. The shock of the event delayed Gair for half a heartbeat. Never had the stallion behaved like this.

"Ibn Bey!" Gair ran after him, but soon halted in his pursuit.

Looking like a virgin beguiling a unicorn, there was Heather. She held her hand flat. Ibn Bey nuzzled her palm, almost lovingly. He took a step nearer to the lass and lightly shoved her with his muzzle, his elegant silken mane, black as midnight, falling forward, draping over her arm.

This was a new experience for Gair. First, he found it hard to comprehend that Ibn Bey had sought Heather out. The horse had been wary to the point of fury since his near death in the desert. He tolerated the company of the Templars only when necessary, shunned all but Gair whenever possible.

And as for Heather...when Gair looked upon her, he was usually focused only on her eyes—eyes that held so many secrets and emotions. But now, he watched her from a distance and in profile. He was not bound by the spell she cast and, for this moment, could examine her at his leisure.

She was not the same lass he had first laid eyes on in the smoky tavern. Her hair had grown and was a luxuriant fall of brown waves, trailing down her back. The thick wool gown of forest green skimmed over fertile curves. Gone was the thin waif-like lass in threadbare rags. In her place was an enchanting female possessed of grace, charm, and soft parts that any man would love to caress. Her breasts were high, firm and round—as were her buttocks. The breeze pushed the fabric of her gown against her, profiling the softness of her belly, the swell of her thighs, legs well formed and firm. No fragile flower was Heather—she was hardy, strong and shimmering with vitality.

The hem of her gown skimmed over delicate slippers. She was no longer a poor, barefoot lass without connection. Henry and his lady-wife had taken a particular liking to Heather, and knowing her link to the weeping stone, Gair knew the house of Sanctclaire would always see she was fed, housed and protected.

Even if Gair failed at the task.

Suddenly a hot sweep of a powerful emotion gripped him. He would not fail. Not this time.

"I will keep the lass safe—no other man but me shall see to the task. Only me." He allowed himself the pleasure of simply watching her and the horse.

Heather smiled at Ibn Bey's nudging. He was a

haughty beast, much like his master. While Gair had been ill, she had gone to the horse. Whether she was seeking comfort just being near the animal that Gair valued, she didn't know, but she had gone nonetheless. And while she was there, a bond had formed between her and the stallion. He was gentle as a dog, easily more mannered than Halt or Hold, so she had taken him to the upper deck each day for a walk in the fresh air. It had taken no time at all before he was following at her heels like the wild things of Ard Na Said. Now he whuffled softly and shook his head, the lovely thick mane shimmering in the sunlight of the morning.

"Braw creature, and you are proud of yourself, I ken that, but with good reason. You are fine." She leaned against his neck enjoying the warmth and the wonderful scent of him. "What would it feel like to ride you, I wonder?"

"When we make landfall and the wedding is done, it shall be my gift to you." Gair said. "You shall ride him each day if that be your wish."

"You travel on cat's paws." Heather had not been aware of his presence but from his words, she had no doubt he'd heard her speaking to the horse. Once again, she was vulnerable to him in a way she did not wish. He knew her inner most thoughts, her secrets and she knew naught of him.

Except for Reza—only his secret love for Reza—something she wished she didn't know.

"Would that please you—to ride upon Ibn Bey?"

"Aye, to do so with my head not covered and trussed up like a pullet bound for the pot would be a fine gift." She stroked the stallion's head. Her fingers sought out the long jagged scar on his shoulder. "'Tis a wicked scar. What wounded the braw beast?"

Gair swallowed hard. He had never spoken of it to anyone. Guiy, Tristan and the other Templars knew part of the story because in a small way they were woven into the warp and woof of the tale. He had sought to bury it far back in the darkest corners of his mind. Now the lass asked, in all innocence, and he was dry-mouthed, wool-tongued and weak-kneed remembering it.

She tilted her head inquisitively at him, the question

burning in her eyes. Those eyes that could pinion him like a barnyard fowl, those eyes that warmed his blood, haunted his dreams and stripped him bare.

He swallowed hard and forced the words to come. "'Tis from a sword blade."

"In battle? You rode him into battle?" There was a tone of censure in her voice that wounded his pride and set his teeth on edge.

"Nay. I was done with trying to purge the world with blood by the time I laid eyes on Ibn Bey." The bitter taste of shattered ideals and lost illusions lingered on Gair's tongue.

Heather blinked at him and turned her gaze back to the stallion. Ibn Bey was happy with her near him, enjoying her gentle touch as she stroked his muscled neck. Gair's mouth grew dryer as he watched those long, slender fingers, pale and smooth against the deep blood bay of the horse's sleek hide. He closed his eyes for a moment and imagined her touching him in that way.

"Forgive me, I dinna mean to pry." She said softly.

He had an opportunity here, but was he man enough to take it? Could he tell her what no other human had ever heard?

"I was sick of blood, sand and hypocrisy. I left Jerusalem and went into the desert. I think maybe I went there to die."

She didn't look at him, she just kept stroking Ibn Bey. The motions of her hands were hypnotic.

"I found myself with a desert tribe. The Sultan of Tazir was a generous and benevolent ruler—he was also was a lover of horses. The finest of the Jedraniah Seglawi line resided in his tents along with his harem."

"Harem?"

"The desert people's customs are unlike ours. A man may take as many wives as he can afford. The Sultan of Tazir was a very wealthy man."

"I ken that means he had many wives."

"He was also rich in daughters."

Reza.

Heather's stomach dropped to the level of her slippers. She wanted to know but she cringed at the thought of him telling her that he loved another. It was on her tongue to ask him to cease—to spare her when he reached out and covered her hand with his own.

"Ibn Bey was hurt when I was... not with him. When I found him later, the wound was bad. It took many weeks for him to recover. When he healed, we joined the Templar knights and their quest."

Relief washed over her. She knew there was much more to the story, more that included Reza but she was glad she didn't have to hear it this day.

"Zeno says we should make land soon." She said softly.

"Aye. Then we will be wed. When you are my wife, all that I possess will be yours. My name, Ibn Bey, my...my..." Words like affection, regard even love hovered at the back of his tongue but he would not say them.

"Your protection?"

Her helpful word allowed Gair to smoothly lie to himself once again. For a moment he considered telling her what was in his heart and mind...but no. He would do his duty to Scotland. He took solace in that steady comforting thought. But when he looked into Heather's eyes—those ever fathomless, never changing eyes—he had the notion Heather was on the edge of tears. But why would the lass be sad to know he would lay down his life for her?

"Aye, lass, you will always have my protection until I breathe my last."

****

The floating islands of blue-ice had become more plentiful, appearing in the sea without warning. Like a ghostly forest, they sprouted up from nowhere it seemed. At first, Hassir thought the end of time had come, but now he understood that Allah was revealing more wonders to his unworthy eyes. It was something he had not conceived of, to see floating frozen islands, many pieces twice the size of the insignificant ship that carried him.

He smiled to himself. Allah had a plan, he was easing Hassir's way to a new world, to justice, and Hassir was sure that plan did not bode well for the corrupt black-robes or the infidels they sought.

Each night after his labors—which were the

lowest and most onerous on the ship—Hassir would wrap himself in his burnoose and pretend to sleep. And when the others settled down with their fermented grape to drink, boast and plan, he would listen.

What he had learned was a confusing puzzle.

The black-robes wanted some valued treasure the other infidels possessed. What was most amazing to Hassir was that the treasure had spent many long years in Jerusalem yet he knew nothing of it. No Sultan had mourned its loss. No cry had gone through the dusty streets when it was taken.

How could there be so great a treasure that none had lost?

A prickling of unease had begun to plague Hassir, and then one night his eyes had popped open and wakefulness crashed upon him. There was one great treasure every man of the desert knew about, one lost and stunning treasure.

Had the Templar-infidels truly found it and spirited it away?

Could they possess the wealth of Solomon's temple?

Chapter Sixteen

The deck rolled beneath her feet, the sun was bright, the air clear and cold. Heather was wrapped in the fine hooded cloak, snug and warm though there were sharp teeth in the wind and a rime of ice on the ship's railing each morn.

Zeno had passed word through the ship that he expected landfall this day but he had said the same for nearly a sennight. Yet Heather had not tired of standing at the railing, along with any man who was not employed in the business of sailing, watching the froth of waves slip by while they scanned the horizon. Today was no different but as they stood shoulder to shoulder, a thick, cloaking fog rolled across the ocean. The white vapor condensed until it obscured the mast of the nearest ship. Soon the mist swirled around Heather's ankles, like serpent's breath , holding her within vapory coils, muffling sound, blurring sight.

The shadowy outline of a man walked by her toward the front of the ship. Soon a ghostly bell began to ring over and over. It was answered in kind, the sound rippling from one ship to another in the world of mist and fog.

"Heather? I dinna find you below. Are you warm enough, lass?" Gair brushed against her as he took up position at her side. No matter how thick the fog he always seemed to know right where she was.

"Aye, I am well." She didn't want her heart to leap each time he asked about her comfort, but it did. "What is the purpose of the continuous ringing of the bells?" She asked.

"In thick fog it is the only way to know where the other ships are. The sound will keep one ship from scuttling another by sailing too near. 'Tis the biggest hazard we face now—fog, shallow water, or one of the ice floes though Zeno assures Henry we are no longer in their path. But if the ship's hull hits a hidden rock near shore it can go under in a wee space of time."

She should be afraid hearing such dire predictions but Gair had hammered it into her head that he would keep her safe. And she believed him. So she was free to let her mind wander. Questions, great and small sizzled through her mind.

What would it be like, this new and undiscovered world?

Would it be a lush Garden of Eden or would it be harsh and cold? Mayhap it would be another giant isle of ice. The thought brought an involuntary shudder.

"Sea-birds will come to us first." Gair was saying.

There was no need to scan the sky, no sign of a winged creature could be seen in this fog.

She sighed in disappointment.

"What troubles you, lass?" Gair's voice, now in a different spot, sent her pulse skipping a beat. It was a never ending source of wonder that a man of his height and bulk of muscle could move with so much stealth she could lose him in the mist. It occurred to her that would make a formidable foe with such a gift.

"I had hoped to be the first to see land."

Her words fed Gair's manly pride. Could she be anxious to become his wife? Or was it merely that she tired of life on a ship? Either way the outcome was the same. The sooner they found Henry's mysterious new country, the sooner he would wed the lass.

"The fog will clear, but remember, the land will not appear as you expect." He stepped up to the rail, standing close to her, inhaling the lovely scent of her. She always reminded him of the fresh, loamy earth of Scotland, a little wild, infinitely seductive, uniquely Heather.

"How so, Gair?"

She glanced up at him, near enough to him that he could see her clearly in the mist, the pull of her gaze made his knees weak. He also realized for the first time that her speech had softened and refined in the weeks since he first saw her on Ard Na Said. She still had a lovely Scot's burr but her manner of speaking was more correct.

She had become a fine lady, if not by birth, then by deed and action. A warm feeling of something very like pride flowed through him.

"Land on the horizon is little more than a ribbon on the surface of the water. Perhaps green, perhaps brown. I know not, for this is Henry's unknown region."

"Has anyone seen this land?" There was a tone of fear in Heather's voice that made Gair's gut clench. Sparing her from fear was almost as important to him as keeping her safe.

"Zeno has charts. The Templars found many scrolls in Jerusalem. Lost for long years, the Order has made certain that a few sea charts were copied and are now finding their way around the known world. Along with a few other copies of relics that are part of the treasure and some artfully crafted replicas of holy objects. They know the secret cannot be kept so they strive to confuse by filling the world with rumors, lies and fakes."

"This voyage of Lord Henry's is based on old scrolls? How can he risk so much on tales that may hold no truth?" Heather's disbelief rang loud and clear.

"I believe in the ancient writings, lass." Henry was almost as light-footed as Gair. He stepped to the rail on her free side. His hair tousled in the breeze, his quick eyes flicking over her for only a moment. "They must be accurate and true. I have risked my name, my fortune, my life on the belief that God is with us. And if God is with us, then who could stand against us? Our quest is just. I have faith."

"Land-ho." The cry rippled through the fog, echoing from vessel to vessel.

Heather snapped her head round. She strained out over the railing no less so than the two tall men at her sides, trying to see through the veil of mist. She followed the line of Gair's finger when he extended his arm.

At first she saw nothing but more of the vapor. A gust of wind caused the fog to swirl. Only the sound of the loose sails flapping was heard for a moment. The mist thinned in spots and revealed the damp, graying deck underfoot. Then the harsh cry of birds filled the air overhead. Heather looked up to see a slice of blue sky.

A stronger breath of wind lifted the strands of her hair at the edge of her cloak hood. Silver and gray wings glinted in the sun as they flew in formation, turned in unison, swept low over the small fleet of rapidly appearing masts.

Like a curtain being drawn, the fog evaporated to reveal little more than a dirty smudge on the farthest horizon.

A new country. An unknown bit of the world.

Heather's heartbeat quickened.

"That...that wee bit of color is it?" Her voice trembled. "That is your unknown land?"

Henry laughed as bells suddenly rang out in discordant but jubilant peals. Manly cheers and whoops of joy rose up from ships scattered out across the sea.

"Och, Heather lass, you have the eyes of a falcon. You have found it! Ah, that wee bit of dirt is New Scotland. No, that name lacks consequence. We shall name it in the Latin. Nova Scotia." Henry swelled with pride.

"Behold, I give you Nova Scotia!" Then he turned on his boot heel and strode across the deck, issuing orders, his body vibrating with purpose and energy, which soon caught like quick-tender, igniting to spread through every soul on the ship.

"Nova Scotia." Heather mused. "'Tis a bonny name."

"The treasure will be hidden anon and we will be wed. Then you, and the treasure, will be safe—forever."

****

The island grew in size as they approached. Zeno guided the vessel, staying well away from the island while every man with a pair of eyes searched for a bay or sheltered cove in which to anchor the fleet. Father MacKee had fallen to his knees and given a blessing. There was a hush while every eye was trained on the vegetation, eager to see if this new world was populated by man or beast. Flocks of pigeons, songbirds, duck, geese and all manner of water fowl exploded from the foliage when the ship came near the shore. Stags and other creatures were spotted further inland, bounding into the lush cover.

"Why do some of the ships hang back, so far behind?" Heather asked Gair.

He looked down at her and for a wee moment, she thought she glimpsed affection in his dark eyes. But it was surely a trick of the light, for when he blinked he had schooled his stern features and the affection was gone like the fog.

"The Gunn Clan will no' land with us. Their ship carries none of the treasure, but many able bodied men. They will follow the coast. Henry craves as much timber as may be had, and other supplies needed to build. 'Tis their task to find and forage."

"And the other ships?"

"Experience has taught us bitter lessons. Henry doesn'a want the fleet helpless, clustered together like young goslings waiting to be picked off by a hungry hawk. We have not glimpsed black sails for a time, but 'twould be folly to think our enemy has given up the chase."

Heather pulled her cloak tighter around her body. It had been so peaceful on the voyage, they world had been so sheltered, she had forgotten the faceless threat they had left behind in Scotland.

A cloud drifted across the sun. Heather shivered as a chill climbed her back. A sense of foreboding settled over her while the ship sailed around the newly discovered world.

****

Hassir slipped the knife inside his burnoose. He had stolen back most of his weapons and the foolish infidels had not even noticed. They had eyes only for the ship they had unexpectedly sighted at dawn. Instead of fleeing, their prey appeared to be sailing towards them, but then abruptly it veered off, sailing south, if Hassir's reckoning of the sun was correct. He doubted the infidels had even seen the black sailed ship in the thin mist of the morning.

The black-robes chattered like women and neglected their duties to look at the sea. A few hours ago, Hassir had felt the ship shudder as its course was altered.

They were giving chase.

When they caught the ship they now pursued like the hawk and hounds of the desert—and he had no doubt they *would* overtake the ship—Hassir intended to escape from these barbarians and see to his own quest.

****

Hassir crouched on deck, every sinew, tendon and muscle tightened, ready to spring. The black-robes were prepared, but not for him. They were focused on the ship emerging from the sheltered cove. The wind was favorable. Sails billowed. Both ship's hulls slid smoothly over the calm water.

Like spiders guarding a web, the black-robes waited, ready to pounce upon the other infidels when they cleared the tidal river and made for open water.

And when they did, Hassir was going to escape.

Suddenly half-a-hundred voices cried out.

A sharp-eyed Scot had spotted the ship with black sails. There would be no advantage of surprise. The Scots were standing on their deck, swords drawn, axes raised. Some beat their swords against the studded shields they carried. They would fight, and Hassir could be free—free to search this strange green world and find his enemy.

He was ready to launch the little boat over the side, prepared to meet the unknown and see if he had the skill to master his own boat, when the deck shuddered beneath his feet.

"Allah, protect me." He prayed.

Loud cracks of breaking wood and shattered joins vibrated through the ship.

The wild-looking Scotsmen's ship had done the unthinkable. They had guided their craft directly toward the black ship. Using their own vessel as a weapon, they rammed the ship. The sound of splintering wood, snapping beams and rushing water was louder than the stunned voices. The sinking craft was boarded in less time than it took for Hassir to free his own blade. The sound of sword meeting shield mingled with screams of agony as flesh yielded to cold sharp steel.

Hassir stared at the carnage before him.

They were all his enemies.

They were all infidels.

He didn't care if they killed each other. By Allah he didn't care. But he found himself brandishing his curved blade. With the distinctive trilling battle cry of the desert he leaped into the middle of his enemy.

****

"Och, you are a braw beastie." Heather rubbed her fingers along the long scar while she stood close to Ibn Bey. He, along with the remaining pigs, goats and fowl were being ferried on a newly built barge to the island. It was a slow process with much squawking, bleating and drama—and the animals were even less pleased than the braying men.

The stallion clearly did not appreciate being billeted with lesser creatures. His nostrils flared, the interior red and moist, while his eyes were white rimmed in excitement.

"He has no liking for these landings. Too many times they have been followed by endless days of running, too little food, water or rest." Gair's voice was rough with effort. Lines were stretched taut on both sides of the simple craft, running from the shore to the ship. He hauled hard on the rope, guiding the barge toward the rocky shore. They had found a place to land but it was no gentle slope of sand, the beach was littered with seashells, weed, and sharp stones.

Beyond, Heather could see the interior of Henry's Nova Scotia, a green, wild tangle of growth. If any foot had trod upon it before, they had left no print or scar of their passing upon the land.

Heather found herself as skittish as the horse. Was it the mysterious voyage or was it simply the prospect of her wedding? She and Gair had not spoken of it—yet. She stroked Ibn Bey, seeking to calm herself as well as the nervous horse.

"Lovely lad, braw beastie, you will have plenty of water and rest this day. There are no battles to be fought—no prize to be won, no plunder to burden you." Heather rubbed her cheek against his neck and closed her eyes.

"I fought no battles for plunder." Gair's low voice brought them open again. "I fought for a cause, for an ideal, misguided as it was."

"I meant no insult." She said softly.

Gair swallowed the dry lump in his throat. Day by day, he became more confused because he wanted her— nay, he didn't want Heather, he told himself.

Only to see her safe. Only to protect her.

Only to do his duty to Scotland.

They reached the shore, and he jumped from the barge while the rope-men on shore secured the lines and set about moving the animals. The creatures were herded to the temporary shelters that had sprung up as quickly as mushrooms after a good rain. The men gamboled after the stock like kids on the heather.

Heather was not as nimble as the men. After many fortnights on the ships, her legs felt wobbly and weak. She was ungainly as she made her way up stiffly up the beach, the wonderful cloak Janet had given her soaking up salt water, weighing her down.

A small army of men from the ships was now on the island, doing a hundred tasks to make their camp secure. The Levite priests had made land a little farther down the shore, building a simple stone alter first, then a great tabernacle of cloth had been erected. The sound of melodious prayer mingled with a sweet smelling smoke and the thud of a hundred hammers. The sharp clang of a blacksmith's anvil soon joined the chorus.

Henry's land was forced to shed the mantle of silence. Birds exploded from the trees, other startled animals darted out and away at the intrusion in their formerly peaceful world. She marveled at sight. Zeno was even busy, bent over his charts, tracing his finger over something, glancing from time to time at the far horizon.

Curiosity nipped at Heather's mind. Gair never spoke of what they intended to do to keep the treasure safe. Did the priests know of some magical incantation from the ancient writings—or was their goal something more tangible? Were they building a storehouse? She had heard the stonecutters say they had found a cliff face that would provide blocks. Truly these men had skills and resources aplenty. If anyone could keep the hoard protected, it was this group of warriors, craftsman and priests.

Safe.

The word had been uttered so much lately Heather wasn't sure she understood its entire meaning anymore. She knew well and good that Gair's only interest in her was not as a lass, not as a lover, wife or possible mother of his children, but as a savior of Scotland.

Someone to keep Scotland secure.

He was devoted to her for that reason alone. And in doing so he had pledged to keep her from harm.

And she was still to learn what purpose fate had in

mind for her. She had expected to know by now. How long was it going to take to find her role—her part in Scotland's history? Or was the myth simply an old wives-tale?

She watched Gair secure Ibn Bey in a small meadow with green grass and a wee burn. Henry was taking long strides up the beach, Halt and Hold nipping at the waves that broke over the rocks and bubbled up near his boots. The Sanctclaire laird stopped and spoke with each man he encountered. Zeno was stacking charts on one of the long tables that had been brought from the ship, scribing something onto a parchment. Father MacKee was kneeling in prayer.

All of them had a task, a duty, an objective on this strange voyage.

"Everyone but me, Lord. What is my reason for being here? When will I know?"

Chapter Seventeen

"The moon is unchanged. Here so far from Ard Na
Said, I expected it to appear different somehow, but it is
the same moon. Who understands these things?" Heather
stared up at the silver orb. She was wearing one of her
thickest woolen tartan gowns and the heavy cloak. Her
feet were encased in leather slippers. Even with the hood
pulled up, she felt the damp coolness of the night. Gair
had offered her the comfort of the ship's dry cabins until
something better was built on the island, but she had
stubbornly refused—driven by an imp that made her
answer sharp and terse. Now he stood beside her, a stout
bulwark against whatever the night might bring. If he
had been offended by her shrewish tongue, he gave no
indication.

It only served to confound her further. For a man
who had once wanted to slay her, he had become eerily
docile in her company. Or was it all a ruse? "The first time
I looked upon the moon in the desert I felt the same. In
such a strange land, I expected the moon to be changed. It
struck me odd that the same moon that shone on
Christendom also shone on the barbarian tribes of the
desert." The heat from their bodies mingled and he caught
a whiff of her womanly scent. A hot and powerful hunger
surged through his blood.

"Aye, I ken your meaning. 'Tis foolish to be
disappointed, but I am."

"What?" Gair blinked realizing he had heard little of
what she said.

"You spoke of the moon in the desert? Is the night
much altered? You have spoken of sand and heat, it is so
at night?"

"Och, no, lass, the desert turns cool. The same moon
that hangs like a fat pearl over our heads, pale, and
mysterious, lights the cold desert night, but there the
similarity ceases. I now ken, 'twas me that was much

changed in the desert, but I dinnae realize it at the time."

"How? How were you unlike yourself?" She wondered if he would finally tell her of his love for Reza. She wondered if she could withstand the heartbreak.

"I learned humility. I grieved the loss of the ideals of my youth. I lost...my honor and other things I held in high regard." Gair looked deep into her eyes. The magnetic pull of his gaze tugged at her. She swayed toward him—her body seeking his heat, his scent, *him*.

Gair's hand moved in a slow tentative fashion. He picked up a strand of hair that had crept from beneath the hood and rubbed it between his thumb and forefinger. It caught the moonlight, held it, shimmering like polished metal. It was in his mind to tell her that the desert had stripped him of all his beliefs and transformed him. He started to tell her that he had lost his love of life, his desire, his ability to give of himself. But if he did that he would be forced to tell her that she was breathing life back into him each day—that she was like rain in the desert—he was like the thirsty dunes, soaking up the moisture, becoming an oasis where things might take root and grow. But he couldn't—because it was only his desire to see Scotland have its heroine that kept him beside her. Naught else.

Naught more.

Naught more than that. He did not care for her. He couldn't.

****

Sunrise broke over the horizon sending night mists rising like vapory wraiths. Fires along the beach had been tended through the night, the smoke thick and gray. The wet salt air and the tangled vines kept the island cool, dim and shrouded in damp. Heather had burrowed into her cloak on her palette inside a rough wee shelter Gair had constructed for her comfort. Now she poked her nose out of her hood and looked about the large camp where, even as men broke their fast with cheese, bread and watered wine at two long tables brought from the ship, they were toiling. Some worked in pairs, referring to scrolls, gesturing at the ocean. Others were digging large square foundations, and yet others waded into the chilled water of the ocean up to their waists, talking rapidly to each other.

"Faith, but 'tis like stirring a den of ants and watching them swarm." Father MacKee yawned and ran his fingers through his thin hair until it stuck out all directions. He walked in the stumping awkward way old men do when their joints are tight. "Do these men never sleep?"

"You wi' have a proper roof over your head in three days time." Gair told the priest. "For that you should give thanks they do not remain abed, priest."

Father MacKee took no notice of the way Gair bit off the word. He yawned again and managed a smile while he stretched on leg like a aging old goat.

"And won't my old bones be glad of that? This new land is wet as Ireland in the spring. And didn't I think we would find something different after so long a voyage?"

"I canna know what you think, priest." Gair raised a brow and shrugged out of his mist-dampened cloak. The morning air was sharp as his words.

Heather raked him with her eyes, powerless to look away. He yanked off his tunic, his chain mail, his hauberk and finally his thin saffron shirt beneath it all. He stood garbed on in only his doeskin trews, his leather cross-garters emphasizing the size and definition of his hard muscled legs.

The morning sun cast pleasing shadows on the contours of his chest. The short curling hair, not red, not brown, but something between, glistened in the light. Her eyes drank him in. She shuddered and took a deep breath, thinking it would steady her, but instead his very essence filled her nostrils, mouth, lingered on the back of her tongue like fine, unwatered wine.

It was like heaven; it was like hell. She was so close she could see the tiny crinkles at the corner of his eyes, she could see the scar near his brow, she could see yesterday's growth of beard.

And yet, she might as well be out on Henry's ship, bobbing in the cove, because she would never know the bliss of having him touch her with loving hands—hands that reached for her and cherished her only.

Reza had left her mark.

The hours she'd spent with him when he was fevered

had given her a taste of what might have been—what could never be. She thought of the weeping stone and its promise that she would love only once.

How unfair it was that she was fated for him alone when he had already given away his heart.

He bent to pick up a wicked, wide-bladed ax, the muscles across his back bunching as he hefted it.

She had agreed to be his wife—in truth was eager to be his wife, but the prospect of needing his affection and never having it was sapping her courage. She was at risk, a part of her fearful of what would happen to her.

And then it hit her. She didn't feel safe in regard to her heart.

With a painful jolt she realized, she would trade safety for love any day. She would risk unknown perils of the flesh just to have Gair adore her. She would trade his vow to see her safe just to hear three words fall from his lips. She would gladly risk heart and limb if she could know what it was to be truly loved for herself alone and not because of a weeping stone.

****

The stonemasons oversaw the men on ropes, straining to load great, square slabs of rock onto barges that were then shoved into the sea. Using all their skill and every available man, the barges had been loaded with the blocks, lime and other materials that had either been brought by ship or procured from the bounty of Henry's Nova Scotia. The great barges were guided into position then with precision, sunk into the sea by the men in the surrounding small boats. When they disappeared into the salt water the slabs of rock that dropped into the sea fitted together until stone by stone a coffer dam was built in the ocean. It took all day but by finally the dam held back the mighty waves that had brought them here.

Heather marveled at the ingenuity of their creation when the surf no longer licked at the island beach in a great arc. Now the waves were far back, lapping at the stone dam, some sluicing over harmless and controlled. Within a few days, the seabed betwixt them and the island would be dry. Then the excavations for the trenches would begin, or so she had overheard one of the tillers telling Laird Sanctclaire.

"And you are certain the design is patent?" Henry asked the master mason that stood stiff as a statue, tensely watching as the waves were held in abeyance. Only when the last barge disappeared beneath the waves and the flow of water changed did he release a taut breath of air.

"Aye, 'tis only the first step of many but now we are free to fashion the water traps and prepare to dig the deep, enormous vaults to receive the treasure. If you would come with me, I will show you the drawings."

Henry glanced up and caught her eye. "Heather, come, look at our plans. You are a part of this venture, and I would have your opinion."

She felt heat climb her cheeks and fought the urge to duck her head—caught as she was listening when not invited. But Henry's gaze held no censure so she squared her shoulders and lifted her chin. "Aye, I would be much pleased to see your plans and understand."

Heather walked beside the Sanctlclaire laird to a table cluttered with scrolls, skins and parchments. One large piece was spread atop many others. It had strange symbols scribed around its edge and in the middle was a drawing. In the center was a temple, then there were marks that looked like a map to a new location.

"I left its twin at Kirkwall." Henry slid his fingers over the hide scroll. "When this work is finished and I return to Scotland, it is my dream to see the Sanctclaire's construct a holy temple in this fashion."

"'Tis a bonny shape."

"It is a rendering of Solomon's Temple." Awe rang in Henry's voice. "And what do you think of this?" He pulled another parchment closer to her.

It took a moment for her to realize she was looking at a crosscut of a deep shaft.

"Here, here and here will lay the lined trenches." The master mason said, pointing at three locations with a blunt finger.

She leaned nearer and scanned it.

"This will be the farthest point." The mason said.

Her eyes went immediately to the lowest point. Notations at the side of the drawing recorded the depth.

"Och, 'tis it possible to dig two hundred feet down?"

She gasped at the thought.

"That and more." The master builder said with pride then he leaned over the drawing. The finger he jabbed at the drawing was callused, the nails short as if broken in hard labor. "Here is where the treasure will rest. At intervals up the shaft we will install certain, shall we call them, deterrents?"

"Deterrents?" Heather was fascinated. "And what would that mean?"

His chest expanded with pride, his thick beard scrunching against his neck. "Look here—at one hundred seventy feet we will leave a sheet of iron, hammered two inches thick. Above that we will deposit but one chest filled with papers that will explain what we did and why should any of our order in the future have the knowledge to open the first of the traps. They alone will have the knowledge to go deeper without peril. At one hundred fifty eight feet, the shaft from the south shore will intersect with this main pit. This is but one of our water traps."

"Do you ken, Heather?" Henry asked, his brow furrowed deeply. "We leave this treasure here with the hope that none will find it until Christ himself returns and reclaims it for his own. But if the Order survives and the knowledge is passed down, there will be some in the world at all times that will know the truth."

She digested his words. Until this moment, she really had no notion of the impact, the dedication, the sheer magnitude of their endeavor. Suddenly she felt very small, but very privileged to be one of only a few who would know the truth of Solomon's missing treasure.

"I ken now. 'Tis a wondrous plan."

The builder grinned with satisfaction. "Here above the water shaft we will leave a layer of clay for stability. Upon that, another tunnel, then an air space. Then we will lay down a stout floor of oak planks thicker than two men's hands."

"Is that why you have dismantled one of the ships?" Heather asked, looking toward the bay were now the bare ribs of a once beautiful craft jutted up like the carcass of a wounded animal.

"Aye. Then above that oak floor, we will craft a tunnel to the cove. There are caves a'plenty below the waterline of this isle. There will be layers of rubble and empty casks, and we will leave a stone inscribed with runes and symbols that only one who is a part of our guild will understand. This will put us sixty feet deep and now the more important water traps and safe guards will be constructed. We will lay down a network of planks and fibers brought for this purpose and by the time we are at forty feet the water level of the tides will be channeled in such a way that any who dig will find naught but a water-filled hole when the morn comes. They will never be able to thwart the design, for the more they dig, the more traps they will open. Every ten feet from there to ground level, we will install a platform of oaken planks. Our engineers and finest craftsmen are certain none will discover the pit's secrets. It has been designed to confound any who would claim the treasure before the Lord wills it."

Heather could but stare at the drawing in awe. She could well believe that none but God Almighty could retrieve what would rest two hundred feet below Henry's isle.

"And if that is not enough, even now in Scotland, France and other places, false trails are being laid. Craftsmen have created duplicates, designed to deceive, of many of the relics. They are whispering in public houses, forging scrolls to confound. One absurd rumor is even being circulated that Jesus may have been wed, ridiculous to any but the most gullible of fools, but just one of many rumors the Order is starting to mask our trail and hide the truth."

"But only a dolt could believe such tales." Heather couldn't imagine anyone with so little faith, or so much gullibility.

****

The brilliant sun burned off the fog and gloom. The island, though rocky and tangled, was a magical place that reminded Gair of the deep highland glens of his childhood. The constant sound of saw, hammer and shovel awakened some sleeping desire inside him. He found himself wanting to build a home, till a field, father a child. He could well see a man putting down roots, sowing the land, sowing his seed in sons and daughters.

He mentally shook himself. Those were dangerous thoughts for a man such as himself. Was he forgetting the bitter lesson learned in his youth? Certain kinds of men, men like Henry Sanctclaire, could have a wife and bairns. Gair was not such a man. He was damned by his brutal past and doomed by past failures to live by his sword. He was a dog to watch at night—an arm holding a killing blade—he had naught to offer Heather but his protection and his binding oath to keep her out of harm's way. That sober logic didn't sooth the raw longing that had been roused in his soul.

He forced those thoughts to the farthest corner of his mind and put his frustrated energy into felling trees. Each man on the island had a task. They employed their skills to best advantage to see the treasure brought to its vault from the hiding places in the holds of the ships anchored off shore. He had not time to squander on wishes and dreams that could never be.

Gair was so intent on the axe eating away at the tree, he was unaware that Guiy had joined him until the French knight spoke.

"*Mon Ami*, has Henri lost his good sense?" Guiy folded his arms over his chest. "I do not understand why you construct the strong, water-worthy barges only with the intent to sink them. Each day I understand you Scotsmen less."

Gair knew Henry did not share his plans and vision with all. Only the master mason knew the entire plan, everyone else had been told only bits and pieces of the whole. He stopped chopping and leaned on the handle of the axe to explain this small thing to Guiy.

"The Romans built such barges, loaded with mortar and stone. They fashioned sheltered harbors. Henry has consulted the masons and their best architects. The great slabs o' granite were sunk to form a bulwark."

"And *viola*, the dam it is built in the sea!" Guiy snapped his fingers. "I begin to see. Perhaps you wild men of the highlands are not so dim as I thought, *oui*?"

"Not so dim as a Frenchman, I am thinking. A coffer dam to hold back the sea is the first step in the builder's design. But I see you and the other Templars are constructing a round keep—what is the meaning of it?"

"Ze round temple—we build wherever we go. They can be found in the loneliest places in France, Germany and on Henri's Orkney. Now there will be one here in this new world." Guiy arched a brow. "Ah, but I also see ze walls and ze roof of a cottage, zat iz your part of the design as well, *oui*? A proper dwelling? Or could it be for some other purpose having nothing to do with ze vaults?"

Gair knew where the conversation was going. He said nothing, only returned to his task of felling the tree, swinging his ax harder and faster.

"Ze stonecutters, they work hard not only to hide the treasure but to provide you with the private chateau. Ze foundation being laid today iz to be ze wedding cottage, iz it not? Ze wedding of ze petite, is on tomorrow's eve, *oui*?"

"*Oui*." Gair swung, the axe biting hard into the tree. The wood cracked, groaned and splintered. "*Oui*, the wedding is tomorrow eve."

****

Heather dressed for the pledging ceremony in a gown of her own making. She vowed to be wed in a garment that had been hers and hers alone. She had worked every spare moment, stitching the gown from the woven goods provided by Gair. Around the neck, she had worked fine thread into a never-ending loop design similar to those she had seen in Kirkwall.

It was a matter of no small significance to her that she was coming to him in more than a borrowed shift.

She was starting her life as a wife with something that truly belonged to her. It meant much to her to come to Gair in a garment that had not come from Lady Janet and Laird Henry's charity.

Over the last months, she had allowed herself to become weak, taking the gifts of Henry and Janet which had been no small wound to her pride.

It was a lack she intended to remedy.

She ran her fingers over the little carved chest full of acorns. Strange that this gift from Gair had not evoked the feeling that she was accepting charity. And when he filled it to the lip with acorns, it was an even greater gift. The wee chest had been the first thing she asked to be brought from the ship when the master builders had completed the braw cottage here on the island. Henry had led her to the threshold, still scented with the clean, piney fragrance of fresh cut timber, and opened the stout door.

"'Tis yours for as long as you bide on the island, Heather of Ard Na Said. And I hope that will be a long, long while." The Sanctclaire had flourished his hand to her. She stepped inside feeling like the veriest lady and had placed the braw chest near the stout stone hearth. Now she stood alone, anxious, shaking with both dread and anticipation as the last preparations were made for the ceremony.

Laird Henry would walk her to the bower where Father MacKee waited with Gair. The blessings would be done by both the priest and the Earl of Orkney. Outlaw Templar knights, secret guilds and Levite priests would put witness to the deed. No other of her gender would be present.

It was a strange way to begin her wedded life. Henry had warned her there would be much merry-making and bawdy jests, and afterward when wine had loosened tongues and lightened heads, she and Gair would retire to this very cottage.

For the bedding.

In a few hours, she would be a wife.

Gair's wife.

She had thought it impossible because she believed him to be a Templar knight, a warrior-monk sworn to a life of solitude and prayer. God forgive her, she was giddy when she learned he had not taken permanent vows. It was what she wanted above all else, to be Gair's wife, to bide with him until death. Whether he loved her not, she wanted him, craved him, would sacrifice her foolish dreams of being loved by him, just to be at his side.

Because Heather harbored a secret hope. She wished with all her might that maybe, just perhaps after enough time and enough living, Gair might come to love her a little as well.

"I pray he wi'."

****

Gair stood with his feet braced apart, his hand on the hilt of his sword. Not because he was ready for battle, not even because Tristan had remarked that it made him look like a brooding warrior, and that a maid might find it appealing—he did it to steady his shaking hand.

Heather was to be his wife.

His heart hammered in his chest, and though he sought to deny it, his belly was knotted in fear.

Fear of words and ceremony. A fright, cold and strong, gripped him, threatened to unman him. How should it be so? He had faced death, barely escaping it, lingering so long in the desert so close to his end he saw the face of St. Peter standing at the locked gates of Heaven, so why should the prospect of a blessing, a promise to a lass and a binding kiss, hold him in such dread?

He couldn't ken the reason. But a small voice at the very edge of his mind knew it. The wicked voice told him he was afraid because he was in danger of losing his heart to Heather.

Nay, he refused to consider such offal. He sought only to protect the lass, and with her, Scotland.

He dinna care. He couldn'a care. He could not allow her to care for him.

Not again, never again.

Chapter Eighteen

"Have a care!" Rufus Gunn shouted.

The splintered mast with the tattered crossed dagger and rood on a field of black began to fall. The battle had been fierce, the bloodshed appalling, but at last victory was in sight. The peaceful tidal river was stained with gore, black garments and dying men floated among the water grasses. The assassins' ship was on fire and heading for the open sea.

"The craven cowards. They left their wounded to drown. Look at them run!"

"They won't gi' far. The flames are licking at the ship. It wi' burn down to the waterline, I trow. I doubt they wi' gi' the flames under control a'fore the big waves swamp her."

"Och, the bloody bastards are like hornets; kill a dozen but a dozen more fly from the nest. And I canna think one ship sailed alone. There must be others near." Seamus Gunn shook a menacing fist at the retreating ship.

"Aye, you may have the right of it. Keep a watch on." The Gunn turned to survey the damage of his own ship. It was scarred and battered but not broken. A voice bellowed from below to report the hull was sound and was not taking on water.

But the ship was not the only thing to consider. The Gunn clan had suffered. Bloody gashes and crippling wounds marred the bodies of more than fifty men. Among the worst of the wreckage on deck was the body of Sir James Gunn of Clyth. He had taken down three before felled himself. Now his mangled body rested in a pool of his own noble blood.

"We must tend the wounded. Then by heaven we wi' sailuntil we find a spit of land worthy to receive James. We wi' bury him and make such monument to him as can be fashioned. Then we must hie to the Sanctclaire with all haste. For if there is one papist ship there is bound to be others."

"What shall we do with this one, Rufus?" Rory held his dirk to Hassir's throat.

Rufus regarded him with narrowed eyes. Hassir could almost hear the man's mind working, trying to divine what part he had played in their attack.

"That one saved my life. I know not what his purpose was, but he killed a papist to save me, he wielded that curved blade of his as if he had slit more than one throat." A bloody Scot said, stepping to the fore.

"Aye, he fought like a demon against the papists." Another one, dripping blood from his shoulder said.

"Speak true. Did you fight for us?" The Gunn asked.

Hassir considered the question. Did he, by fighting his captor's aid these men? Allah had put him on the side of these rough creatures.

"I fought against the Black-robes."

The Scotsmen the others called Rufus raised one thick, reddish brow. Then he smiled grimly.

"The enemy of my enemy is my friend. So be it, give this man ale, bread and make him welcome. We will let Laird Henry decide his fate."

Hassir was not bound, but he was watched as carefully as he observed the Scotsmen.

"Drop anchor!" Dougal pointed to a sheer rock face. "That is a fitting place to bury James. We can carve his name upon yon stone."

"Nay. We will no' leave his name. We will leave his bones and in the rock we shall carve his image, with the Clan Gunn device upon his shield. Let those who have eyes to see know who he was and the rest of the world be damned!" Rory brandished his sword to a loud cheer that rippled through the men.

Hassir watched in silence as the men bathed, regarbed and armed their fallen friend. With solemn respect they laid him on a plank and loaded his corpse onto a small boat.

"Come, you will stay beneath my gaze until your fate is decided." Rufus Gunn told Hassir.

One man played a mournful funeral dirge on a pipe that wheezed and moaned like an old woman in a dust storm. It surprised Hassir to witness such regard and feeling. Until this moment, Hassir had not credited the infidels with heart, or honor, but he knew their misery was not feigned. This gave him much to consider.

It took some time for the men to find a place to beach the boa that pleased them. Then with the same hushed reverence the Scotsmen picked up the board with their kinsman's body and started the long climb up the hill. The way was not easy or short but they did not complain or waver in their task. When they reached a level ledge, they set about hacking out a deep hole with their battle axes, no easy feat in the rocky soil. Hassir sat with his back against a stone, watching, contemplating. It took hours but as the sun dipped toward the west, the body of the fallen warrior was laid to rest. Prayers were said, this surprised Hassir most of all, for they were not so different from the prayers he had said over the body of his cousin. Then several men climbed the rock and using a rough drawing on a skin as a guide they set about making holes in the cliff face. It was sometime before they all finished, the sun was nearly set, but Hassir could see what they had crafted.

On the solid rock was a crude but mighty outline of the dead man. In one hand was a sword, on his other arm, a shield with a ship, a center mast with a sail tied up, and above the mast hung a star. At each upper corner were circles intersected by lines—perhaps they were moons, Hassir did not know. It was then he realized that all the heathens carried shields with odd designs. One was clearly three boar heads. Another was a fist holding a crown. Another was a serpent in combat with what appeared to be a white rooster. Strange words wreathed many of them.

"You clearly have an unspoken question on your lips." Rufus said. "Ask it before it chokes you."

Hassir wanted to remain silent and aloof, but he was curious. "What is the meaning of the creatures on your shields?"

Rufus held his shield up. "They are our lineage. In battle one man looks like another, so we have devices that tell who we are and from where we hail."

"Ah." Hassir said nodding. He cast back in his

memory. Had his enemy carried such a shield when he trod the desert sands? If he did, Hassir could not recall it. He wasn't sure why but learning these things about the barbarous men left him with a nagging sense of disquiet. He was better able to hate them when he did not know these details of their lives. It was easy to yearn for their deaths when he had not witnessed their grief and shared in their ceremony.

He was a troubled man when he went to prayer. Allah, the merciful, the mighty, the benevolent had sent Hassir into a confusing place.

****

"Let us raise our voices to the Lord Almighty." Father MacKee held his palm over the clasped hands of Gair and Heather while the wedding blessing was said. There was not a breath of wind, no fowl or furred creature stirred. It was as if this moment were frozen in time.

Heather took the opportunity to gaze up at Gair through her lashes. He looked stern, braw beyond a maid's dreams. Suddenly as if he felt her eyes upon him, he looked down upon her. They stared into one another's eyes. She saw a flicker of something hot, primal and potent in his dark gaze. Whatever it was, it was answered by the beat of her heart and the flush that climbed her body, ending at the roots of her hair.

"And would you be repeatin' after me?" Father MacKee asked in an ordinary voice, as if eternity had not passed in the last few moments while Heather was lost in Gair's eyes.

"I pledge my heart, my trust, my fidelity to you and you alone."

Heather and Gair's voices blended in solemn chorus as they spoke the words together.

"I will cleave only onto you as long as I live, I will laugh with you in good times, weep with you in poor, I will nurse you in sickness and celebrate with you in health."

They repeated the words, and the import of what was happening settled upon Heather like the thick fogs that had surrounded the ship. She couldn't breathe. Panic rose inside her.

Run! Run! A voice in her head bid her flee from this

before—

"Heather." Gair's smooth, deep voice rolled over her. "Lass?"

She glanced up. He was regarding her with an expression that squeezed the last breath of air from her lungs. She was going to swoon.

"Go on lad, kiss her." Laird Henry's voice cut into her paralyzed mind.

"Heather, we are now wed." Gair winced to hear a tone of relief in his voice. "May we not seal our binding with a kiss as 'tis the custom?"

She could do no more than nod. And then she was gathered into his strong, hard arms, swept against his wide chest, held there with gentle steadiness.

When his lips swept over hers, she was at first embarrassed with all the Sanctclaire task men and the guildsmen and the Templars staring. But within a breath her mind ceased to function. Her body took over, answering Gair's kiss, deepening it, questing for more. She forgot where they were. She forgot who she was. Her tongue darted into his mouth, she explored the heat and passion that waited there. Her hands slid up his shoulders and met behind his neck. There her fingers toyed with silky strands of his thick hair.

If this is what it felt like to be wed then it was wonderful. Her terror of a moment ago was forgotten as she lost herself entirely in Gair's embrace.

"Come lass, let us drink our health and then we wi' withdraw." Gair said softly.The word conjured images of dark passion, privacy and the sating of curiosity. Heather knew not what awaited her in the marriage bed, but if Gair was at her side, then she was anxious for the journey.

In short order, cups were passed and blessings toasted. Father MacKee lifted his cup many times, the end of his nose growing redder with each limerick he constructed as he thought of ever more creative ways to intone God's blessing on the nuptials.

"Enough of this!" Guiy slammed his wine down on the rough planks of the table. "'Tis a crime against all reason to keep a groom standing here drinking with his fellows when he has the, how you say, the *amour* waiting."

Gair's lips curled up at the edges, and for the first time in Heather's memory, a bit of mirth lit his eyes. It wasn't a big smile, nay, 'twas small, but it transformed his stern face into one of humor and warmth and let her glimpse a Gair that he kept hidden.

Heather felt her face heat when he swept her up in his arms and strode toward the stone house. He had just reached the door when a cry went up among the men. 'Twas no cry of celebration but a shout of horror.

"*Mon Dieu!*"

"The Gunn ship."

"They are flying their pennons low. Someone has died."

Gair halted and set Heather gently on her feet. He touched her cheek with one finger, tracing a line that set her heart pounding and her eyes drifting closed.

"Ah, lass, you are a temptation." Regret and a deep hunger colored his words.

"Och, and who is this man?" Tristan's harsh voice brought her lids fluttering open. "A man of the desert?— not something you see every day in a new and undiscovered land."

Gair spun on his heel. He strode to the center of the ring of men, elbowing his way through with Heather trotting in his wake. Whatever had drawn Gair's attention was surely worth seeing.

He pushed his way to the front at the very moment a man, swathed in a dark robe and turban, turned to look upon him.

"By Allah, at last we are face to face. By my beard, draw your blade, infidel, make peace with your God for today you will surly die. Vengeance and justice will be mine in the name of my kinsmen."

Chapter Nineteen

Gair drew his dirk from his boot and held it at the ready in front of chest.

"I, Hassir Ibn Falad Rashid, nephew of the Sultan of Tazir, cousin of the murdered maiden, Reza, challenge you, defiler of virgins..."

A strange, taut expression gripped Gair. The tip of his blade lowered a fraction while the dark-skinned man spat insults in his face.

"Thief of horses..."

Gair's weapon lowered a bit more. He no longer stood like a warrior ready for battle. Now he looked—broken.

"...Slayer of maidens. You will die like the dog you are." Hassir vibrated with hatred. It didn't seem to matter to him that he stood among several hundred Scottish warriors, Sanctclaire task men and Templar knights. His fury was unleashed and he hurled one vicious abuse after another.

Beyond reason, at these last words, Gair lowered his weapon totally. His eyes were haunted. Heather stared at him and remembered the moment in her cottage. He had been ready to murder her. Had he done so before? Was he a man that killed women? Did this strange desert man know of past victims?

"Reza will be avenged."

Heather heard the name and her heart plummeted. Here on this new land she had managed to push the woman from her mind. But now, this man had brought her name and her memory, and the harsh question of whether Reza had been Gair's lover or his victim.

"You are Reza's cousin?" Gair's eyes narrowed. "Are you also a kinsman of Abadah?"

"Nay, my mother was the Sultan's of Tazir's sister. Reza and I ran up dunes together as children. She was sweeter than the rain, more constant than the sand. And you shall die for killing her."

Heather's intake of breath brought Gair's head around. He regarded her for a long moment. There was a deep sadness in his gaze—a sadness that brought hot, stinging tears to the back of her eyes.

"You killed Reza?" She whispered.

Gair's voice broke. "Aye. As surely as if I held the blade that took off her head. I had sworn to keep her safe at the request of the Sultan of Tazir. The one task that generous and honorable man asked of me, and I was unable to fulfill his wish. My lack wrought her destruction."

Gair slung his dirk to the earth and turned on his heel, stalking toward the thick, tangled forest.

"What twist of words is this?" Hassir held his blade ready even though hundreds of infidels glared at him. "No twist of words." Guiy stepped forward. "You have come on a fool's errand. Your petite cousin met her fate not by Gair's hand."

"Bah, the story is well known. He admitted as much, though his tongue is like that of the serpent. The Sultan's favorite stallion and his youngest daughter were taken by the infidel."

"*Non.* The Sultan's daughter rode the *bon chevalier*, Ibn Bey. My brother knights and I found Gair in the desert. He was quite...alone."

"What? What is the truth of this tale, then? By my beard I will know of it this day." Hassir shouted.

"'Tis a tale of murder and butchery, but you will not have ze truth from me. You must get it from Gair. For he alone knows the whole story. We know only the bitter and sad end. Now, *mon ami*, give up the blade before we offer you a taste of Templar steel."

Hassir glared at Gair's back as he kept walking, disappearing into the trees. With an oath he slung his curved blade to the ground. It clattered against Gair's discarded dirk.

"I am at your mercy." Hassir extended both hands, wrists together as if he expected to be bound.

Henry arched a dark brow. "You will not be tethered. But I wi' have your oath that you wi' not seek blood from Gair while you are among us."

Hassir frowned. Then he nodded sharply. "If Allah

wishes it. I will not seek his life while we are on the island. But I would know more of this story." He cast a steady look toward Guiy and the Templars.

Tristan cleared his throat. "We have kept our portion of this secret for too long. 'Tis time everyone learned the truth of what happened in the desert."

"By Allah, I would hear of it. Tell the tale and then let me see justice done."

"Justice and revenge are two sides of the same coin, iz zis not so? You may not be so eager to spill blood when you learn the truth." Guiy said.

Henry Sanctclaire cleared his throat and drew the attention of all, including Heather. "You will not speak of what you know, Frenchman. The truth of what happened is Gair's story, to keep or to share. No man on this isle will utter a word until Gair wishes it. This is my decree."

Silence fell over the group. There was no sound of axe, hammer or saw. Laird Henry brow's pinched together. By his look and his status, he dared any man to gainsay him.

****

"Gair?" Heather struggled to follow his path through the tangled of woodland vines. As foolish as it was, she found herself noticing the kinds of trees, the flowers. She counted many varieties but not a single oak among them.

"An isle like this should have a grove of oaks." She muttered just before a root caught her toe and sent her sprawling onto her hands and knees. She gathered her hem, struggling to rise when strong hands grabbed her waist and set her back on her feet.

"Have a care, lass." Gair's rough voice flowed over her like a warm breeze. "Why are you here?"

"Is it not the duty of a wife to follow her husband where'ere' he may go?"

"You are still a virgin and not bedded. You may yet escape disaster. I was a fool to wed you." Gair took a step back as if trying to put distance between them.

Heather's heart plummeted to earth. This was her greatest fear, that he did not want her.

"And if I should not wish to escape?"

"Show sense, Heather. I'm no man to shackle yourself to. My promises of protection are like dust in the wind.

Thank God Hassir arrived to remind me of my lack."

"What happened to you, Gair? What happened to challenge your faith and break your spirit? Was it the desert girl, Reza?" Heather could not believe him capable of murder, no matter what he said.

"My spirit was broken before I met Reza. My faith had been shaken by what I had seen and done in the name of the Christ. I was sick of war, blood and sand. I walked into the desert seeking ...I canna know what I sought—perhaps the release of death. The Sultan of Tazir took me into his family."

"And you repaid my uncle's kindness with treachery." Hassir's voice brought them both spinning round. The man's dark eyes snapped with hatred. "The Sultan's horses were his pride—along with his daughters. Reza was a woman with a child's heart. Her greatest joy was racing across the sand on Ibn Bey. You stole him, infidel. He is a treasure that shall be returned to my uncle's tribe."

For the first time, Gair showed a flash of anger. "I stole nothing."

"Then how do explain his presence here in this wretched land, across the seas, far away from his desert home and the sand that bred him?"

Gair turned away from Hassir once again. He reached out and took hold of Heather's hands. He looked into her eyes, the force of his gaze sending her pulse racing. It was strange, she should be afraid of the man who glared at Gair but she wasn't.

"Henry's fleet wi' soon be returnin' to Orkney. Only he and the builders and a few task men will remain here. The ships wi' sail on the morrow. I want you gone, Heather. I want you to go back where you belong among the heather and the crags if Ard Na Said. Forget you met me, forget all that has happened. Your life and your destiny are in Scotland."

"Our being wed—?"

"Forget that as well."

"But you vowed to see me safe."

"I am keeping that vow—by sending you away from me, the Templars and the treasure."

Chapter Twenty

"Hold fast!" A Sanctclaire task man was in charge of ferrying barrels of fresh water to the waiting ship. The island was bustling, both with the builders at the shore and the preparations being made for the fleet to sail. Heather stood on the pebbly shore, wrapped in her cloak, numb to the fog, and the raw rent in her heart.

Gair had broken her.

She no longer cared if she was a savior of Scotland or the ruin of this expedition. She cared for nothing.

"Heather?" Father MacKee touched her shoulder. It took too much effort to turn and look at him, so she didn't. She simply kept staring at the ships, bobbing like ducks on the waves.

"Are ye ill? Faith, but there isn't a bit of color in yer cheeks." He stepped in front of her and thereby filled her field of vision. She blinked and waited for her eyes to focus.

"Father."

He was the same; small, bright, bird-like eyes and yet, he seemed changed. Or was it simply because she no longer looked at the world in the way she did yester-eve when she still thought things might turn out a 'right.

"Child, come and sit down. Let me fetch ye some ale. Did ye break your fast?"

"Aye. Nay. I canna remember." Heather allowed the little priest to lead her to one of Henry's tables. He shoved aside piles of paper and scrolls. In the blink of an eye, he had bread, cheese and wine before her. "Tis not ale, but wine might be for the best—unwatered, aye, am I not knowin' the grape will put pink in yer cheeks?"

Heather accepted the cup and put it to her lips. She didn't taste the liquid that trickled down her throat, nearly choking her when she failed to swallow. She was so tired. It took too much effort to swallow—it was almost too much effort to pull breath into her body.

She hadn't the energy to gainsay Father MacKee when he broke off a bit of bread and cheese and bade her eat it.

Around her, the flurry of activity went on unchanged. The sound of the hammers and axes had become such a part of the fabric of the island that she didn't hear it anymore. But she did hear the snap of a stick underfoot. She heard the rasp of armor against wool, felt the electric charge in the air and knew without a doubt that Gair was nearby.

Her mouth went dry. Her belly knotted. Her heart skipped.

"Father."

Gair's voice was low, it rubbed over her flesh. He dinna sound well.

"I needs must beg a boon."

"Of course, lad, and wouldn't I grant anything in my power?"

"Pray watch over Heather on the journey to Scotland."

"Faith, and won't ye be watchin' her yerself?"

"Nay, I am no' returning to Scotland. I will bide here with Henry for the winter."

Heather heard the sound of him leaving. Her battered heart went with him whether he wished it or no.

Gair didn't go far, just within the cover of trees where he could watch Heather. She rose from the table and picked up the casket he had given her. Then with her head held high, she walked into the woods.

He kept pace with her, far enough away he was sure she didn't know he was following. Then she began to plant the acorns. One by one, she plucked one from the chest and planted it, then she moved on to do the same, toiling alone, carrying the small coffer full of oak seeds. From time to time, he saw her swipe at her eyes and he knew she wept.

It tore the heart out of his chest to know he was the cause. Yet he sought to spare her any further misery. For he was not a man destined to know happiness. Hassir had been sent by the Lord above to remind Gair of his failings. Just as his promise to keep Reza safe had ended in sorrow, he was convinced that to keep Heather with him would only bring her to destruction. So he watched and mourned for a life he could not have with the lovely Scottish lass that had stolen his heart.

****

Heather rose before dawn. She had slept little, assaulted by dreams, startled by imagined sounds. At one point, she thought she heard Ibn Bey neighing in alarm, then a while later, she imagined men whispering just beyond the barred door of the stone cottage.

It was a dream of fear because she no longer had Gair to protect her.

She donned a warm woolen gown and cloak. Her belongings had been packed and loaded onto Henry's ship last eve. Zeno would be the pilot on the return voyage to Scotland. The remainder of the fleet would once again follow him. Most of Henry's ships would remain in Orkney, but Henry's flagship would return to Scotland—with her aboard.

Heather drew in a deep breath and thought of Ard Na Said. It would be winter soon, and she had no provisions. The specter of hunger and want raised its head.

She had forgotten about such mundane problems while in the company of great men on a momentous quest. Now she realized she must once again see to her own survival.

"Lass, I would escort you to the ship." Laird Henry himself spoke to her from the other side of the door.

She lifted the strong wooden plank from the arms that held it. Henry pulled the door wide, sunlight flooding into the room. She had expected a day of fog and gloom to match her mood.

"The sun doesn'a care where it shines, lass." Henry said as if he had read her thoughts. "You may feel dour inside but God is in His heaven and the world will come to rights. I promise you that."

She managed to hold back her tears. "You are a great laird but no' even you can make such a promise."

"Och, and 'tis wounded I am to hear you have so little faith in my abilities. I wi' be returnin' to Rosslyn in the spring and I expect you to be there to apologize for your hasty words."

"I wi' return to my cot—"

"Nay, lass. You are now, and will continue to be, under my protection. The Templar knights have instructions to see you safely to Rosslyn. Janet will welcome you with open arms."

Heather thought to gainsay him but he held up a hand and said, "I will hear no arguments. You may not believe it now, but you may trust me to do right by you in all things. Now let me take you to the ship. Zeno is anxious to catch the morning wind."Scant moments later, Heather climbed into the small boat and settled herself. She was surprised that it was only the two of them and Henry himself picked up the oars and pulled hard. There was no lull in the activity on the island. She scanned the shore, the site where the Templar's round stone building was being erected, and the tables where many of the guild masters stood, pointing, gesturing, speaking in loud excited voices. Halt and Hold barked and raced back and forth across the beach, alarmed that Henry was not taking them.

She had not seen Gair. A part of her had hoped he might at least come and see her to the ship.

"Have a care climbing the rope." Henry pulled the oars in and handed her up toward the drenched hemp skimming the lapping waves. "And remember, Heather, you may trust and depend on me. Always."

Within moments, Heather was aboard, watching the small boat return to the shore. Henry leaped out of the craft and hauled it up onto the shore, the big hounds plunging in and out of the surf, barking in happiness.

It was all happening so fast. She barely had time to blink before Zeno barked orders, and the sails were unfurled. An obliging gust of wind caught them, filled the sails. The great ship shuddered. Then they were off, heading back to Scotland.

She stood at the railing and watched while the island shrank to the size of a fly-speck, and then disappeared completely. It was like waking from a dream. She could hardly believe any of it had been real. The treasure, the island, the wedding."By Saint Kessog, I will gralloch each and every man that laid hands upon me! Where is my dirk?"

She whirled around, her breath caught in her throat. That voice. But it couldn'a be.

Gair staggered up the steps from below. A length of rope was still coiled about his body, frayed strands dangled from his chaffed wrists. His eyes were dark with rage and blood lust.

"Where are they?" He roared.

"Who?"

"Those French swine and Laird Henry Sanctclaire! Where are they? Their jest will no' seem so amusin' when I put my dirk to their necks. Show me where they hide, woman."

Heather pointed in the direction where she had last seen the island. Nothing but blue water and white capped waves could be seen in all four directions except for the ships that trailed Henry's great craft.

"The Templars are on board with us—Laird Henry is still on Nova Scotia."

"The island?" He blinked and rubbed at a large bump on his forehead. "Henry remains—and I am here...with you...sailing home to Scotland? This canna be."

Heather nodded while her heart tumbled inside her breast. Laird Henry had said she could trust and depend upon him. Now she understood what he meant. He and the Templars had put Gair on this ship with her.

It was a long way back to Orkney. A long journey and much could yet happen. She clung to the tiny shred of hope and concealed her secret smile from her angry husband.

****

"Easy my lad." Gair untied Ibn Bey's tether and prepared to walk him up the ramp to the upper deck. At least the Templars had taken care with the fractious stallion. Gair knew it couldn't have been easy for them to handle him but there was not a mark upon his sleek hide—except for the old scar. For that kindness, Gair could almost forgive them their other sins—almost.

He had been betrayed by the very men who espoused brotherhood. Now he was trapped on the Scottish bound vessel—with Heather. Just knowing she was aboard had brought erotic dreams and fevered wanting. Ibn Bey was restless as well, fighting the lead as he trotted up the ramp for his exercise. Gair happened to glance back into the dim hold when a movement caught his eye. He drew his dirk from the sheath below his knee.

"Come out, I have felt the burn of your eyes on me and I know 'tis you."

A shadow unfolded itself from the darkness. Hassir Ibn Falad Rashid stepped into the bar of light. Heather had been watching Gair from a position on the bow. She stepped into the shadows behind a barrel of fresh water to listen and watch to the two men, praying they would not kill each other.

"I should have expected you to stow-away like a rat." Gair nearly growled.

"Allah has once again brought us together, infidel. I have prayed much, and he has revealed to me that I cannot kill you until I have heard the fullness of your tale."

"Then you are doomed to a life of disappointment for I wi' no' speak of what happened." Gair sheathed his dirk then slapped Ibn Bey on the rump. They trotted away leaving the desert man alone.

A shiver ran through Heather. Though the reasons were different, she was as curious as Gair's enemy about what happened in the desert. She slipped out from her hiding place and approached Hassir.

"But how shall we loosen his tongue?"

"You should stay far away from him. He is a defiler of virgins and slayer of maidens."

The desert man stood tall, erect, lean as a reed with a manner that made her think of the turban on his head as a crown.

"I am his wife."

"Wedded by your custom but yet a virgin."

"How can you know such a thing?"

"I have sharp ears like the desert fox."

The shame of her virginity washed over Heather. It was true her wedding had not been consummated. She wanted to blame this man. If he had not shown up wishing harm to Gair, she might now be with him on Henry's isle. He suddenly swept up the hem of his voluminous garment, gathered it to his middle and bowed deeply at the waist.

"I am Hassir Ibn Falad Rashid." He straightened and inclined his head, his small, dark beard catching the sun that played hide and seek among a gathering bank of clouds. "I have no quarrel with you, and I give you my oath that I will do all in my power to keep you safe after I have taken your infidel husband's life."

"I am Heather of Ard Na Said...and Gair's wife. If any man shall keep me safe 'twill be him for I canna think you wi' find him so easy to slay or you would have seen to the task long ago." Heather studied him for a long moment while a flush crept up his swarthy face.

Then a great shout of alarm went up from another ship. Bells pealed, men shouted. She whirled to see another vessel bearing down on one of the guild ships. They seemed to touch each other. Both crafts shuddered, and then the sound of steel on steel reached Heather's ears.

Suddenly Gair was beside her, Ibn Bey dancing at his side. The horse's nostrils flared and Heather was sure he recognized the sounds of war.

"Heather, get below." Gair barked at her. He caught her by the elbow and started to lead her and the excited stallion down the ramp into the dimness of the hold.

She went with him for half a step and then something inside her snapped.

"Nay." She planted her feet and jerked her elbow from his grasp. "Nay. As you ha' said, over and over, I am not bedded and still a virgin. I have been kidnapped, trussed up, ordered around, and told where to go for far too long. If I am not your wife, then I canna be expected to obey you as one."

"What folly is this?" Gair looked stunned.

"I say nay. I willna' go below."

"But...'tis no' safe for you here."

"Life is not about being safe, Gair. 'Tis a lesson you should have learned long ago. If I have a destiny to fulfill, then I wi' be about it. Trying to be safe does not suit a savior o' Scotland."

"But Heather, lass...you must no' be reckless wi your life. With your stubbornness you court folly. I canna let harm come to you. I canna allow you to be hurt like...""Were about to say like Reza?"

"Nay—nay." Ibn Bey was straining at the lead. Gair glanced from the stallion, to Heather, to Hassir who lingered nearby unconcerned about the fate of the other ships.

Worry, pain, and something dark flitted through Gair's eyes. "I canna—nay, I willna' speak of Reza."

"Then I willna' move from this very spot." Heather took a step backward. From the corner of her eye, she saw more black sailed ships engaging the Sanctclaire's fleet. It was only a matter of time before they reached the lead ship.

"At last you show good judgment. You are wise to resist the infidel's counsel." Hassir complimented Heather. His eyes gleamed in what—triumph? A part of her wanted to deny him, to tell him that she was Gair's in body, mind and spirit, but a small voice told her this was the time to take a stand. She risked all with this bold move, but she could no longer acquiesce to Gair's wishes—not if she had any hope of being his wife in name and deed.

"Whether my judgment be good or ill, 'tis mine to use, desert man."

A kind of wild desperation filled Gair's face. He whirled on Hassir, the stallion strained against the tether, the sounds of battle wafting over the waves, growing closer, ever closer.

"Ibn Bey shall be safe if none else is." Gair rushed down the ramp to the hold below. Heather's heart sank. She had hoped, but evidently, Gair would never shed the bonds of the past by speaking of what happened.

She turned away and hid her face from the dark scrutiny of Hassir. Then she heard rapid footfalls coming back up the ramp. Gair emerged, his face mottled in fury, his hands clenched into fists.

"You wish to hear of Reza? Then I shall tell you both. And damn you for it!" Gair spoke through clenched teeth. He stood on the deck, the wind ruffling his hair.

"By Allah, at last." Hassir crowed.

Chapter Twenty-one

"I came into the desert a broken man, tired of war, blood and death. The Sultan of Tazir was a man of generous nature. He welcomed me to his tents, took me into the bosom of his family. And all he asked of me was one thing; to keep his youngest daughter safe."

Safe. Heather had begun to hate the word and all it signified.

"Reza was wild as a gazelle and beautiful as the lotus blooming in the oasis. She and Ibn Bey were inseparable—the Sultan's two greatest treasures. I knew that Reza had developed tender feelings for me—"

At this Hassir winced. His hand twitched. "By my beard—"

Gair cut him off with a glance. "But I had given my vow of honor. I did not bed her, Hassir. She was untouched by me. The Sultan had in mind for her to marry Abadah, but Reza wanted naught of him. And so the Sultan was going to let her have her infatuation, then when the flame of her first loved burned out, he intended to break with tradition and allow her to choose her own mate."

"You lie." Hassir hissed. "He would not have broken with the customs of our family."

"I dinnae touch her, and I do no' lie. The Sultan had married all his other daughters off with an eye to wealth and status. It was his desire to see Reza marry only for love."

"Bah. I do not believe it!"

"We will never know who Reza sought to wed for her father died and Abadah came to claim her as his bride and her family's wealth as his own. Reza evaded him and rode off into the desert on Ibn Bey. I gave chase, still bound by the oath I had sworn to the Sultan to see her safe."

"The ship is upon us!" Zeno yelled while the crew

moved in unison to prepare for battle.

"Finish the tale, Gair." Heather urged, praying the ship would not overtake them too soon. "I pray thee, tell me. Tell me all."

He glanced at the black sails then his gaze returned to Heather. "I followed Reza and found her at the well. Ibn Bey was tired—she was resting him. I let down my guard and Abadah's men were upon us. I fought them and Reza escaped—I foolishly thought she would be safe."

"Abadah took you?" Hassir's brow was furrowed.

Gair's lips twisted in a grimace. "Aye, he took me. Beaten senseless, I woke buried up to my neck in the hot sun. Abadah had entombed me in sight of the well so I should see water as I died of thirst. The sun came and went while I roasted. Two days, maybe three, I lost count. My tongue dried and swelled out o' my mouth. My skin blistered. I prepared myself to meet God."

"And yet you are here." Hassir's words dripped with venom.

"Aye, I was found by nine Templar knights. They freed me, tended me, and I survived. When I was in my right mind again we went to find Reza."

Silence hung in the air. The wind had picked up, waves were rising high, white foam riding each one.

"You found her?" Heather prompted.

Gair turned to her again, his face a mask of pain, horror and guilt. His voice was dry, harsh. "Aye, I found what the jackals and butcher birds had left of her. She had been—beheaded. It had been done from horseback, the blow so vicious it cut through Reza and down into Ibn Bey's shoulder. He was standing over her body, their blood had mingled in the sand. All because I failed at keeping her safe."

It was at that moment the sound of shattering wood drowned out Gair's voice. Heather whirled to see great treble hooks of iron fly across the span betwixt them, the tridents dragged until they bit into the wood. Even now, men used planks to board Henry's ship.

Gair drew his sword and shoved Heather behind his back. "Lord above! Take my mortal life this day, but I beg You, keep the lass safe."

Hassir fell to his knees and put his forehead upon the

deck. "Allah, the merciful, let me show these infidels how one of the faithful dies." Hassir leaped beside Gair. "Let us put the maid between us and defend her to the death."

Heather could see nothing but their backs while they provided her with a living shield. She had little choice but to stand there and listen to the sounds of hell come to earth.

****

Heather opened her eyes to darkness and a searing burn in her shoulder. Her head pounded and it hurt to breathe. All around her was sound, but her brain couldn't separate the voices into words. She didn't move as she tried to take stock of her surroundings and clear her head. Her garments were soaked, smelling of the sea and the coppery wash of blood. She shivered with cold but when she tried to lever herself up from the deck her arm wouldn't hold her.

She was aware of another's breathing next to her.

Who was it? Who shared the deck?

Plucking up her strength, she turned her head and peered into the darkness. A chill breeze swept over her and then a drift of clouds parted, moonlight spilled over the deck.

"Gair."

He lay beside her, unmoving. Was he breathing? The pain took her breath but she rolled herself toward him. Her frigid fingers touched his face.

He was yet warm.

"Heather." The sound of Gair's rough voice made her heart skip a beat. "I canna move, canna rise. Am I skewered?"

She couldn't answer. Blood stained the deck. Was it all his?

"I fear he iz how you say, near *morte*, death." Guiy hovered nearby. He was so calm and detached that Heather wanted to shove him over the side.

"Lassie," Gair's rough voice tumbled over her. Then he broke her heart in twain when he reached up, put his wide palm at the nape of her neck and pulled her lips down to his.

The kiss filled her with heat, driving the chill from her bones and the fog from her mind. On her knees now, she buried her hands in the folds of his plaid and melted onto the hard muscular chest of her husband. His warmth flooded through her while her soul sang with joy and withered with sadness. Now, he would kiss her and know her for herself—now, when he lay dying?

"By Allah, do you infidels have no sense of how to behave? No man of the desert would allow his wife to behave in such a manner under the gaze of other men." Hassir criticized.

"I am no man of the desert. I am a highlander, with a Scottish wife who has my leave to do as she wishes."

Gair's voice was surprisingly strong. Heather had the vague sense that he was rallying. Did she dare hope he might not die?

"Ha, a wife you do not want, a wife you cast from your bed still a virgin." Hassir taunted. "There is no pride to be had in that."

"Hassir, is it now your intention to harry me onto my death with the sound of your voice? Kill me now and have done with it."

"You are in no condition to fight me, Scotsman. Blood stains the deck where you lay. I cannot slay a dying man, and in truth, Allah compels me to offer up my apologies while you yet breathe. I believe you did not defile Reza, you did not steal the treasure of the desert, Ibn Bey. You should go to your death knowing this."

Heather couldn't breathe for grief, and this man talked of the past! Who cared? Not she with the aching heart. Gair was dying. She clutched his hand and bathed his face with kisses.

"Ah,'tis a rich man who is sent to Allah with the kisses of his beloved on his lips." Hassir said. "If only you could let go of the past and realize you did not fail Reza you would journey unburdened from this life."

The clouds covered the moon, when they parted it was to reveal the distant sparkle of stars. The ocean was a flat black surface silvered with writhing bars of silver moonlight.

"What, have you nothing to say?" Hassir stood with arms akimbo, his swarthy face mysterious in the shadowy light. "You will breathe your last with that prideful burden still clutched to your bosom? The men of your bloodline have no sense."

"Cease!" Heather could no longer hold her tongue. "Do not torment him. Leave him in peace. Have you no heart a'tall?"

Hassir only arched a dark brow.

"Sweet Heather. If only—" Gair winced as if in pain. "I ha' been a fool, lass. I should have taken you to my bed, and made you my wife in all ways. 'Tis a sad thing for a man to leave nothing of himself behind but regret."

"Ah, so now at the hour of your death you would embrace life and leave the foolish guilt in the desert where it belongs?" Hassir's white teeth flashed in the moonlight.

"Aye, I would shed my guilt and my regrets. If I had a few more days—hours even—I would make sweet love to my wife and pray to get a babe upon her." Though Gair spoke to Hassir he stared into Heather's face. He kissed away her tears and caressed her with his gaze. His hands were steady and strong upon her.

Hassir tipped back his head and laughed. The mirthful sound shocked Heather. She wanted to flail him with her fists.

"How can you be so cruel?"

"*Non*, petite, ze man iz crafty but not so cruel as you may think." Guiy stepped up and looked down at Gair. Then he roughly nudged him with the toe of his boot. "You will not die zis day. Rise, rise and take your bride."

Heather struggled to her feet, her arm ached and throbbed. She flew at Guiy and beat upon his chest with one closed fist. "You barbarous Frenchman! How dare you?"

Guiy grabbed her wrists. "Look, ma petite. Ze man iz rising—I tell you ze wound iz not mortal. A scratch upon his leg—no more."

Gair was on his feet, swaying like a drunkard, with a look of murder in his eyes. He grabbed Hassir by the shoulder, the laughter dying in the foreigner's throat when Gair pulled him around nearly nose to nose.

"What wickedness is this?" Gair roared.

Hassir smiled, his straight white teeth flashing in the moonlight. "The Templar knights and I tired of this foolishness. The blood belongs to the black-robes we slew before we sent their ships to the bottom of the ocean. I carry with me the dried petals of a potent desert flower—it causes weakness—for a time. But you need have no fear. When the affects wear off it will not impair your ability as a husband."

Heather blinked at Hassir's words. Guiy, Tristan and François were all grinning. Suddenly she realized what they had done.

"In front of God and all these witnesses, you have sworn to take me to be your wife in all ways." She murmured.

Gair shoved Hassir from him. He blinked and turned to her, a lop-sided grin graced his face.

"Och,'tis true, lass. I ha' been a great fool and yet I canna set aside my need to keep you safe."

"Gair, I realized long ago that I would trade safety for love. And what better way to keep me safe than to keep me at your side?"

His grin turned to laughter, the sound deep, rumbling as it bubbled from him. He took a lurching step toward her. His face twisted in pain and he looked down at his leg in surprise. "A scratch you say?" Blood was running freely.

"Perhaps a bit more than a scratch, eh? Alas, *mon ami* the wound you suffer might keep you abed?" Guiy waggled his brows. "Shall I tend your wounds as I did in the desert, *oui*?"

"Nay, you shall no' touch me, Frenchman!" Gair looped an arm around Heather's shoulder. "Are you hurt, lass?"

"My shoulder hurts."

Gair gently peeled back the torn fabric. There was a nick in her flesh. His face was a portrait of rage, compassion, and finally, love.

"Come, lassie. We will tend each other. I wi' wash your body and you wi' wash mine. And then I am going to treat you as a husband should."

Chapter Twenty-two

Heather and Gair stood on the Scottish beach and waved at the retreating ship. Ibn Bey pawed at the pebbles and broken shells, impatient to be off to graze among the heather. Aboard the ship, the Templar knights, their white tunics concealed beneath brown cloaks, waved back.

"Tis sad to see them all go, but at least they know what their place in the world shall be."

"Och, lass do you no' realize your place in the world?"

"Nay. I ha' done naught that is bold or good for Scotland."

"How can you say so? You found the cup and, by doing so, saw it restored to the treasure. You journeyed across the water and planted a grove of acorns that wi' one day be mighty oaks."

"Naught of that was good for Scotland."

"You are wed to me." He grinned.

She hit him softly in the chest with her fist. "You are forever making jests, I ken I liked you better when all you did was scowl."

"Nay, you dinna'."

"Will Guiy and the rest be hunted?" Heather asked her husband who held her close with one brawny arm looped around her shoulders.

"They sail to Cypress where they have a great holding. They are a canny lot. Now that the treasure is safe and Henry is returned, I canna help but believe all wi' be safe."

"I will miss them, much as they raise my hackles."

"Aye and Hassir too."

Heather tipped up her face and looked at Gair in disbelief. "I wi' not miss him."

"No matter how his journey began, I wi' forever be in his debt for helping to protect you and I canna hold a grudge, if he had not fed me the potion and made me believe I was dying I canna say I would ever have found the sense to take you to wife. 'Tis a sad thing, lass, but I no' a quick-witted man."

Heather didn't answer. She gazed after the ship. "There is one thing I still don't understand, Gair."

"Aye, lass?"

"Why dinna the Templars simply reveal the treasure to the world. Would it not be wondrous for all to know of it and every event it signified?"

"Ah, but don't you see, lass, if the treasure would have been revealed it would be proof, solid, irrefutable proof of Jesus' life and death. It would be like those who dinna believe in the flood finding Noah's great Ark."

"I dinna ken."

"Faith is believing in the absence of proof, Heather. God doesn'a need to prove—we need to belief and have faith."

"I think I finally understand."

"Now, if you ha' no more questions, there is one other matter I needs must attend."

"Aye?" she answered softly.

"Aye. 'Tis in my mind to tell you what I should have done long ago."

Heather could not imagine what Gair was talking about.

"'Tis time I told you, Heather of Ard Na Said, I love you. Forever and a day, my lass, for as long as there is breath in my body, I wi' cherish you."

Then he bent and kissed her lips. The Scottish wind sighed and filled the sails of the retreating ship.

Author's Note

While this book is a work of fiction all events portrayed can be backed by scholarly research. Ard Na Said is riddled with caves and the legend of Arthur and his men sleeping beneath the mound is well known in Scotland. Salsbury Crags is a shoulder of rock, shrouded in mystery, home to all the creatures mentioned.Henry Sinclair was a Laird of Scotland and the Earl of Orkney, where an age appropriate scroll has recently been found depicting what appears to be both Solomon's Temple and Rosslyn Chapel's design.

Rosslyn castle, while now in ruins, was a wondrous keep, without question there were vaults large enough to hold a great treasure. At least five tunnels branching off into the rocks beneath the site, led to the spot where the chapel was eventually built at least ninety years before Columbus sailed for American. Carved in stone are both maize and aloe vera, new world plants that had been seen long before the Santa Maria made the voyage. The Zeno documents support the legend of the voyage made by Henry Sinclair.

Oak Island does indeed have a diabolical shaft, constructed as described in this book. A drilling bit brought up evidence of gold. So far nobody has been able to thwart the water traps that protect it, nobody is sure who built it or why, but one inescapable fact remains; whoever did construct it was a master builder and there is no doubt it hides some secret meant to be kept. Scholars argue that only the Masons could have built such a canny hiding place. There is evidence of at least one Gunn Clan member on North American soil. The likeness of a knight, complete with age appropriate armor and a shield with the Gunn clan devise resides on a cliff. Other artifacts have been found in the area of Nova Scotia to support the theory that Henry Sinclair, in the company of Templar knights made a voyage to the new world long before Columbus.

The rest of the story is entirely from my imagination and hypothesis based on several years of research.

Linda L. Crockett writing as Linda Lea Castle

A word about the author...

Linda Castle aka Innis Grace lives in northern New Mexico, and is well acquainted with the towns that dot the Rocky Mountains. As Linda Lea Castle she has written fourteen historical romances for such publishers as Harlequin and Kensington, and is an award-winning, internationally renowned author. Her books—which have seen publication in multiple languages—are known for their history, mystery, faith and inspiration.

Visit Linda at www.lindacastle.net